The Secret of the Coconut Groves

by G. H. Teed

A Wonderful Tale of the Copra Industry, introducing Sexton Blake, Dr. Huxton Rymer and Mary Trent.

First published in the Sexton Blake Library—
30 June 1925. No. 1. (New Series (2nd)).

Stillwoods Edition, 2019.

Stillwoods.Blogspot.Ca

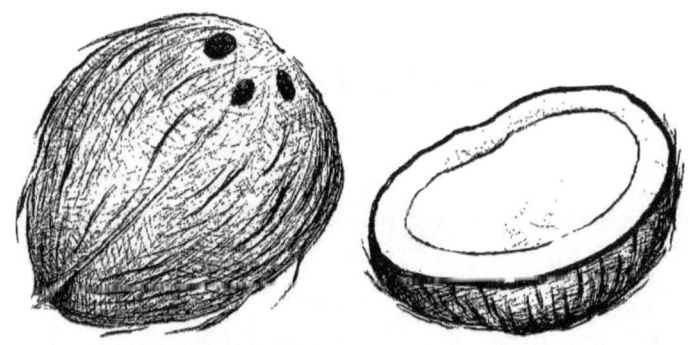

Coconut

Catalogue Information:
Title: The Secret of the Coconut Groves
Author: G. H. Teed (1886-1938)
First Published: Sexton Blake Library—
30 June 1925. No. 1. (New Series (2nd)).
Cover adapted from the original by Arthur Jones
This Edition: Stillwoods, 2019.
ISBN Canada: 978-1-988304-69-4
Blog: Stillwoods.Blogspot.Ca
Author's Blog: http://ghteed.blogspot.com/
Storefront: http://www.lulu.com/spotlight/lulubook22

Keywords: fiction, detective Sexton Blake series, Mary Trent, Dr. Huxton Rymer

Doctor Huxton Rymer is always looking for the easy money. In this story he arrives in Cochin, India with Mary Trent after their small ship flounders in an adventure. Here he finds a coconut pearl and this gives him a new idea.

But as so frequently happens, the master detective, Sexton Blake and assistant, Tinker arrive at the same location to assist with a copra business.

Suspense and thrills follow the heroes and villain in exotic India.

N.B. – There is a small glossary at the end of this novel.

Author's Note.

IT is widespread knowledge that, aside from the true pearl or salt-water oyster pearl, there are also to be purchased in any pearl market gems known to the trade as "culture pearls." These culture pearls are, from every test, actually genuine pearls, but they are not produced altogether through the accident of Nature, as ordinary pearls.

The latter are caused through a small bit of sand or gravel getting into the oyster and setting up an acute irritation. In order to get over this and confine it to one spot, the oyster automatically produces a sort of fluid which gradually is built round and round the irritant spot, and in time forms what we call a pearl. These pearls, so formed, may be of all shapes and sizes, and, according to such grading, are valued in the pearl market.

Culture pearls, on the other hand, while formed in the same way, are begun by the insertion of an irritant, or even a small seed pearl, into the oyster by the hand of man, and this industry has recently reached very extensive proportions in Japan. Aside from these, there are, of course, the fresh-water pearls, caused in the same way in the rivers of China, but which have only a nominal market value; also the naturally-formed fresh-water pearl of the Mississippi River, in the United States. Again, one finds imitation pearls, the product of the laboratory, in the shop windows of every city and town, but these are frankly not what they are represented to be, and can easily be detected.

But, in addition to these various forms, there is a pearl formed by Nature which is rarely found, and which, when it does come to light, commands a very high price in any market, for it is one of the most beautiful creations of Nature, and as genuine in every way as the salt-water oyster pearl. This pearl is known as the coco-nut pearl, and may be called actually a vegetable pearl.

How is it formed? By the same type of process which forms the salt-water oyster pearl. Everyone who has ever lined up at a coco-nut shy[1] will have noticed, whether he has won a nut or not, that in one end of each coco-nut there are three round dark spots, through one of

---

[1] A coconut shy (or coconut shie) is a traditional game frequently found as a sidestall at funfairs and fêtes. The game consists of throwing wooden balls at a row of coconuts balanced on posts.

which access can be gained to the "milk" inside, for the filling of that hole is soft, and easily pierced. Well, it is common knowledge that Nature often indulges in freaks, from eggs with double yokes to two-headed calves. And that is exactly how the coco-nut pearl arrives. This soft spot on the nut is that through which the young shoot of the coco-nut comes when it is sprouting. It is the only way in which it can emerge from the nut, and should that be closed it must turn back upon itself and subsist on its own "meat" until it dies.

Occasionally, very occasionally, it is true, this hole is not sufficiently soft to permit the tender shoot to grow through. The nut is a freak nut, formed with that spot filled with a hard, impenetrable substance, owing to a rare disease that has attacked it. On failing to get through the young shoot, as has been said, turns back upon itself, and this sets up an acute irritation within in exactly the same way in which irritation starts in a pearl oyster.

The result is the same in each case. Nature, in order to heal the spot, produces a sort of fluid which is wrapped round the place, so to say, and which, as growth progresses, increases in size and hardness until a pearl is formed. Every man who knows this (and there are not very many) is always on the watch for just such a freak nut, if it is his business to handle them, and, needless to say, if he finds the natives of the district ignorant of this, he does not enlighten them. It is said that if one could read the secret of the disease and apply it to a large number of trees, the proportion of pearls so produced would be very large, and would soon run to an enormous value. It is probably due to some chemical reaction which takes place in the mud in which the roots seek their nourishment, and through them the tree becomes inoculated.

The author of this story lived for four years in the Malabar Coast of India, one of the most extensive coco-nut producing districts on the globe, and can vouch that the above is fact. Hence the following story built on those possibilities.

The End of the Author's Note.

Photo by A. Hyatt Verrill.

CHAPTER 1. Mutiny—Rymer versus the Crew—A Desperate Fight.

THE rush came aft along the deck before Huxton Rymer even suspected that rank mutiny was afoot. There had been unrest among the native lascars for the past two days, and a certain amount of muttering at the long hours which the different watches were forced to spend at the pumps.

But two days before Rymer had explained with far more trouble than he usually took, and far greater patience than it was his habit to display, that, if they valued their own lives, it was necessary for them to keep the pumps going, or they would find themselves afloat on the Arabian Sea in a boat which was not large enough to hold everyone on board; which meant that two or three would have to be left to flounder about in the broad ocean wastes as best they could; and he made it quite plain that he and the "missy sahib" would most certainly not be included in that number. Which was fair enough, when one considers the risks and perils of the sea.

But rank mutiny! He had not expected that. In fact, he had not considered there were enough "guts" in the whole caboodle to kick up more than a weak protest. If he had guessed such a thing was coming, he would have, and could have, settled it in the usual way, with fists and feet and a belaying-pin, if necessary.

But as a bunch of plotters they certainly deserved credit for the way in which they had kept their intention secret until the moment came to spring it.

And so the rush came aft along the deck while Rymer was struggling with the wheel of the schooner in the fluky sweep of a nasty squall—these had been hitting them with irritating frequency and persistency ever since the day before—and when he had not even Mary Trent beside him to take the wheel while he dealt with the mutineers.

Mary Trent had stood the morning watch beside him, as well as having taken her turn during the night, and it had been at Rymer's sharp insistence that she had at last gone below to get some sleep.

In a way, he was glad she was not on deck when the rush came, and, at the same time, the thought of a white woman on the schooner, at the mercy of those black devils if he should go under, was just the spur which the mutineers had not reckoned on, for they did not know the very special niche Mary Trent occupied in the life and thoughts and work of Dr. Huxton Rymer.

Rymer had no time to lash the wheel. As he saw the mob coming along the waist he guessed quickly enough what was up. Every man-jack had picked up a weapon of some sort, and there was that in their eyes that told their intention.

There were fourteen of them in all in the crew, and the whole fourteen had joined in the conspiracy.

About six miles off the starboard quarter lay the South Malabar coast of India, and just about opposite where the schooner was beating at that moment, Rymer knew the Travancore town of Alleppey lay. But it might have been as far distant as Rangoon for all the good it did him.

He knew there wasn't a sail in sight, nor a plume of smoke to mark the passing of some steamer. He had seen nothing since the previous afternoon, when a low-lying pattimar had passed them, bound south, probably to Colombo.

He had just himself and his own brawn and wits to depend on, and, while he had a shrewd suspicion that Mary Trent may have already been locked in her cabin, he let out a loud yell as the mob came on, and then, at imminent risk of the schooner capsizing with the wheel banging free, he clawed out his heavy service revolver and jumped to meet the mutineers just as they reached the poop.

There was no time to parley, and Rymer knew it. This mutiny, it was plain to see, was all cut and dried, and nothing he could say would deter them.

So, with the full authority of his position behind him, he opened up with the gun. He did not make the mistake of shooting low just to wound in the limbs, nor of shooting high. He was a crack shot, and he aimed to get his man with each shot.

And, as the black wave came over the edge of the poop, he sent one, and a second and a third, crashing back into the waist, each man with a bullet clean through his heart.

Three! Three out of fourteen, which left eleven still to deal with. And he knew he had three more cartridges left in the chambers.

Rymer was no kid-glove gentleman, as is well known, and it didn't worry him in the slightest that he had had to shoot down three of the mutinous crew.

It was the old story of the survival of the fittest, and he knew perfectly well if he didn't "get" them they would get him. Which was a thing he had no intention should happen if anything he could do would prevent it.

And, to do him justice, if the toll he had already taken had held them for the moment he would not have shot again until forced to.

But it didn't. They came swarming on to the poop, and one of them sent an iron belaying-pin flying with deadly accuracy at Rymer's head.

Rymer saw it coming just in time to dodge, but even at that it flicked his ear as it flew past and plonked into the sea astern. His white teeth showed in a snarl as his pointed black beard parted, and, even with the foremost of the mob almost within fondling distance, he coolly picked off two more.

That made five, leaving nine to deal with, and he did not use his last cartridge, for it was an old maxim with Rymer, as with most experienced campaigners, that one should always have one cartridge left for a last emergency.

Just at that moment the schooner heeled over dangerously, and the great boom came sweeping across the deck as she almost jibed.

The lurch, and her subsequent recovery, sent several of the mutineers sprawling and almost threw Rymer to the deck. But he was the first to recover himself, and, jerking off the white topee he had been wearing, he flung it full into the face of the man nearest him. Then he clubbed his heavy weapon and started in.

It was a great fight. Rymer caught one of the blacks a smashing blow in the face with the butt of the revolver, and the fellow went down with a crash, being flung by the next roll of the schooner against the rail, where he lay.

By this time the gang had recovered itself, and, seeing that the big white man had already put six of their number out of commission, they realised that they would have to bear him down quickly, if at all.

Ordinarily, that mob would not have had the courage or the initiative to cook up such an attack. But among them was one of those scheming gutter-sweepings which sailor-men know as a sea lawyer, and it was his conniving brain that had devised the whole plot.

Rymer was aware such an one must exist, but the trouble was to pick him. If he had known, the first bullet would have been his; but he realised that, so far, he had not "got" him, for the crowd was still held by the determination to finish the job. So there was nothing for it but to reach for the nearest.

Another lurch of the schooner, and Rymer realised that the whole lot of them would be in the sea if the wheel was not taken soon.

He knew, too, that Mary Trent must be locked in her cabin, or imprisoned in some way, for she was enough of a sailor to know that something must be wrong by the wild lurching of the ship. Had she been free she would have been on deck before now. And that was an added worry to Rymer.

Another belaying-pin came flying at him, and this time it caught him heavily on the left shoulder, almost numbing it.

He fixed the man who had thrown it and rushed for him. Then the whole mob, like a swarm of bandicoots, was upon him and over him and about him, and, as their arms clawed for him, as they smashed in their weapons with wild cries, Rymer went seafighting mad.

He used the clubbed revolver; he used his left fist; and he used both feet. He even used his head. And it is a safe bet that that bunch of lascars, many the fight though they might have seen in different ports, had never seen a white man in full action as they did then.

Rymer was a wild, fighting fury. He was like a bull attacked by a horde of many curs. He towered in the midst of them while they clawed at him and struck at him with their weapons. And then he laughed! He gave a great roar, but it wasn't mirth. It was a danger signal which they would have done well to heed. But they didn't.

They stuck to him like a fell disease. And Rymer fought. He slugged and slogged and kicked and butted and drove the heavy weapon into this face and that face. He heaved this man up and hurled him bodily a good two yards away.

He broke the clawing hold of another at his throat, and snapped the black arm like a pipe-stem. He took a terrific blow on the side of the jaw with another mirthless roar, and smashed the skull of the man who did it.

He suddenly dropped down in a crouch, and when his mighty shoulders broke through again he was clutching the leg of another. He heaved back by sheer force of his weight. He broke free for a moment, and then even those lascars paused as he swung his captive round as if he were handling a leg of mutton.

Around once the helpless black was whirled. Around twice, and still a third time; and then, with another roar, Rymer let him go. He sailed out and across, and struck the side with a terrific impact. From four yards away, and with the flapping of the sails in their ears, the watchers could hear the sharp, tell-tale crack as the fellow's neck snapped.

And then, while they still were held in this new dismay, Rymer was into them again. He gave them neither rest nor pause. He asked for no quarter, and he gave none. He hit them and smashed them and flailed them. He drove them back to the edge of the poop and into the waist.

He picked up still another by the middle and sent him flying a dozen feet away to fetch up like a sack of bran against the main-mast. Then they broke; and, once having broke, they fled.

Rymer gave them no rest. He hurried them forward, and he drove them back along the waist. He flailed them forward again, and he would have hunted them into the darkest corner of the fo'c'stle if the schooner, at that moment, had not given a wild lurch, and then heeled in such a way that it seemed she must capsize.

Rymer, knowing that victory was his, turned and raced aft. He had no fear that they would think he was in flight. Their casualties were too heavy for that.

He braced and watched the schooner pick herself up and respond to the helm. Then the boom came over, and she steadied. It was a nice bit of seamanship, carried out just in time.

And then, as he had time to gaze forward again, Rymer saw that those of the mutineers who were still on their feet were talking together in the waist, and he knew some fresh plan was brewing.

CHAPTER 2.   Deserted by the Crew—The Sinking Schooner— A Race against Time.

RYMER was not left long in ignorance of their new plan.

There were, by count, just five of them, with two men lying wounded or with limbs broken (still another, one of the five, had his arm snapped), five dead by shooting, one with his neck broken against the side, and one with a smashed skull, where Rymer had clubbed him with the butt of the revolver.

It was a pretty heavy list of casualties for twenty minutes fighting, and still the lone white man stood on his feet—bruised and battered but still standing.

In about five minutes Rymer saw what they were up to. The whole crowd suddenly disappeared into the fo'c'stle, but reappeared soon after carrying what they could of their belongings. At that, there wasn't much to carry, for the Lascar is not exactly what one would call a luxurious traveller.

They dumped these down by the side, and, while three of them stood guard, keeping a wary eye on Rymer the while, the other two caught hold of the two wounded men in the waist and dragged them along to where the little heap of belongings lay.

Rymer still stuck to the wheel while two of them undid the falls of the only boat the schooner carried and lowered it into the water.

Even then Rymer did nothing. He had seen what their intention was, and at first he had made as if to abandon the wheel and go forward to drive them back into the fo'c'stle. But he changed his mind and simply gazed cynically at them while they dumped their belongings into the boat and lowered away the two wounded men. Then the others got in, and, releasing the falls, pushed off.

They were swept past the stern a few seconds later, and, as he looked over at them, one of them stood up, waving his arms and shouting something unintelligible, but which, it was easy enough to guess, were intended as threats.

Rymer did not answer, but in this man he knew he had found the ringleader of the mutiny, and he marked the fellow well in case he should ever see him again. He saw them take up the oars, and, after one who was in the bow pointed towards the distant shore and said something, they settled down to row, and as the sea wasn't very high, Rymer figured they ought to make the coast safely enough.

Only then did he leave the wheel. With the schooner running along fairly well, but, as he could see, getting still lower in the water, and acting to every touch slowly and sluggishly, he knew perfectly well that she could not keep afloat many hours.

But he wasn't going to give up the fight until he knew it was quite hopeless, and he had seen too many craft flounder along for hours on end and still keep afloat, when, by all the laws, they ought to have gone under.

His first care was to see if Mary Trent was all right. In order to go down below he would have to leave the wheel, but he caught up a length of rope lying near at hand and lashed it against the binnacle.

Then he turned his attention to the seven dead men. He confirmed his opinion first, but found that appearances had not deceived him. They were as dead as stones, and with very little ceremony, Rymer dumped them over the side, one after the other.

He saw that the mutineers in flight in the ship's boat had stopped rowing and were watching him, but they made no attempt to come back, knowing as well as Rymer knew that their misguided fellows had paid the full penalty, and that they would be sharks' meat before many minutes had passed.

Then Rymer went below.

He made straight for Mary Trent's cabin and called her. She answered him from within, and, after assuring him she was all right, asked what had happened. Rymer did not answer until he had got the door open, and then, as she rushed out to him and caught hold of him anxiously, he laughed.

"I was worried about you, my dear," he said. "I thought those dogs had probably fastened you in your cabin, and knew you would wonder what was up when the schooner lurched about so crazily."

"Yes—yes," she said. "But what has happened?"

"We had a little difference of opinion," he answered. "It was the same old trouble about the pumps. They were apparently convinced that the old tub could not be kept afloat much longer, and the sight of the shore so near at hand was too much for them. So they cooked up a nice little mutiny. I hadn't a suspicion of what was afoot until they rushed me."

"And then?"

"They have decamped—gone over the side, and have taken our only boat with them," he responded. "If you come on deck you will be able to see them, for they are still in sight."

"But the fight—I heard shots and sounds of an awful struggle," she persisted anxiously. "And you—they have struck you, for your face is bruised and your neck is cut."

Rymer patted her arm.

"It was just a nice little entertainment," he said. "It was just what I needed. Now we are alone, and it is up to us to get this schooner into port single-handed or else—"

"Yes?"

"Well, we have the option of running her ashore and trusting to luck or of trying to make some sort of a raft."

"But a port! We can never make Bombay if she is still filling. It must be eight hundred miles away!"

"It is, but that isn't the only port. I could run into the coast here and lie off Alleppey, but that wouldn't do us much good, except that a shore boat might pick us up before she sank under our feet. But that doesn't suit my book, Mary. We have a hundred tons of good Mauritius sugar in the hold, and I am going to save it if I can. I didn't gamble the whole night with that drunken fool of a half-caste skipper back in Mauritius and win his leaky old hooker and her cargo just to have it sink under my feet after sailing it the whole way up through the Indian Ocean to the Arabian Sea. Oh, no! We shall still fight."

"But a port—I don't understand. Isn't Bombay the only harbour into which we could make?"

"Not quite. There is Marmagoa, for instance, but that is too far as well. We could never make it. I could have done so if those scurvy dogs had stuck to the pumps, for she wasn't making water very fast. But that is out of the question. Yet there is another, and it isn't much more than thirty miles from here."

"What is that?"

"Cochin. And that is what I am going to try and run into."

"But I thought ships had to lie offshore just the same as at these other places on this coast?"

"Big ships do, and coasters usually do. But a small hundred-ton schooner like this can get in all right if I can take her through the Gut. It is only a matter of three hundred yards or so wide, and only a portion of that is channel for navigation. The tide rips in and out of there like a millrace. I have seen it and I know. But native sailing craft make it, and they have been making it for hundreds of years. All the pattimars along the coast and from Bombay and the Persian Gulf get in and some of those pattimars are as large as this schooner. So why shouldn't we?"

"Quite true, my friend. If it can be managed, I am sure you will do it—if we can keep afloat."

"That is just the rub, my dear, and from now on you will have to stick to the wheel while I work the pumps. The water will gain even then, but I may be able to keep the old thing afloat until I get through the Gut at Cochin, and, once through there —well, it is soft mud bottom, and very shallow, so I can simply let her run aground. Now, come up on deck, for she is beginning to kick up her heels again."

So this strangely assorted pair, the notorious adventurer and the girl who had thrown in her lot with him, and yet who were both full of the pluck of their race, climbed the companionway where Rymer unlashed the wheel and gave Mary her course. She had looked over the side, and the ship's boat was still near enough for her to see the figures in it. She counted them, making only seven, and at that she looked at Rymer.

"Did all the crew leave then?" she asked.

"They did," he answered curtly.

"But I can only count seven in the boat." she went on. "And there were fourteen altogether."

"Your count is quite correct, my dear," responded Rymer. "Nevertheless, the whole fourteen went over the side, so don't worry your head about them any longer. Now, here is the course."

And Mary Trent, sensing the truth, and nothing more, although her eyes travelled once again over those broad shoulders which had born the brunt of the struggle.

"His code of ethics may not appeal to many, but, thank goodness, he is a man," was what she was thinking.

As soon as Mary had taken the wheel Rymer went forward to the pumps. He took the depth of the water in the well, and got a slight chill down his spine as he found it had gained several inches since the early morning. However, as he had said to the girl, he was not going to abandon his prize without a struggle, so he set to work, and for the next two hours he stuck at his gruelling task.

Nor can Rymer be criticised for his decision. It was quite true, as he had remarked to Mary Trent, that he had won the schooner and her cargo at Mauritius in gaming with her skipper and owner. He had won it through the medium of the dice to be exact, and had completed the deal by beating up the skipper when he would have gone back on his bargain.

The crew he had inherited; and, as he was more than anxious to get away from Mauritius without any loss of time, he had accepted them as they were.

He had good reasons for flitting, for he and Mary Trent had been stuck in that island in the Indian Ocean with nothing to get along on except what Rymer could pick up by his wits. This had been just enough to keep them going, but at no time had he been able to get enough ahead to buy a couple of passages away from the place.

Then the half-caste skipper had fallen into his hands, and, not only did he win something which would take him away from the island, but he found her well stocked with provisions, as well as some ready money in the skipper's cabin.

More than that, he had won her cargo as well, and that was no less than a hundred tons of good Mauritius sugar. The papers were all ready for clearing, and the cargo loaded, so Rymer thought he could do no better than carry out what had been the intention of her late owner—to make for India, and dispose of the sugar in the Bombay market, where there was always a fair price to be had.

But going up the Indian Ocean they had struck foul weather. They had been beaten about and harried hither and thither until the schooner had sprung a leak.

Then Rymer's troubles had started. He had forced the watches to do extra time, and had kept them at the pumps every hour of the day and night, for he carried a master's certificate, and he was seaman enough to know that he was going to have his work cut out for him to make his destination.

His mistake was in sailing up the Arabian Sea in sight of the west coast of southern India. There were green palms, and there was dry land and safety, and it had been too much for the crew of native lascars. They had pleaded with him to run the schooner aground while he could—a request which Rymer had curtly turned down.

Then two days later, without the slightest warning, they had rushed him, and no one knew better than he that they would have killed him if they could, would probably have done worse to Mary Trent before destroying her, and then would have run the schooner ashore to abandon her at some lonely spot or, if they were questioned, to tell some trumped-up tale about the skipper having died at sea.

That was the position on the day when the trouble had broken out, and now, with the mutinous crew, or, rather, the remnants of it, in full flight for the shore, Rymer was left to get the schooner into port the best way he could, with only Mary Trent to assist him.

Very early that morning he had spotted the big coast lighthouse at Alleppey, and knew he was off the Travancore coast. He knew the coast intimately, for he had been in Malabar many times, and he knew that some forty miles further north he would pick up the smaller lighthouse at Cochin.

If he could steer his course for that, and if he could manage to work the schooner through the narrow Gut which gave access to the backwater, then he still had a gambler's chance. And being just what he was, Rymer was determined to take that chance.

At four o'clock that afternoon Rymer spotted the mark for which he was on the look-out. After studying it through his glasses for a few minutes, he hurried below and looked up the current run of tides. Then he took the wheel from Mary, remarking as he did so:

"It's just half on the flood tide now. It will be running through the Gut like billy-o, but we shall have to risk it. The wind will drop at sundown here—it always does, and we couldn't get in against the outrush of the ebb. That backwater drains more than a dozen rivers in a stretch of under a hundred miles, and every blessed drop comes through that Gut.

"Alternatively, if we stick out to-night for the next flood tide, we shan't be afloat to make the attempt. So dig us up some tea, my dear, and we shall have something to eat before seeing what Fate holds in store for us this time."

And with a cheerful little lilting laugh Mary Trent, who hadn't the least atom of fear in going through whatever Rymer suggested, tripped forward to the galley and began foraging about for tea and something to eat.

Rymer ate his by the wheel, and by the time they had finished the Cochin lighthouse was plainly visible about three miles away.

The sun was already dipping low in the west, and Rymer gazed enviously at a low pattimar that had come down the coast and was making for the Gut, which was his objective.

Already her oddly-shaped sail was being furled on the single boom which hung at such a narrow angle against the forward sloping mast, and, even as he watched, she blurred against the dark green of the coconuts on Vipeen point, the upper side of the Gut, then she swept into clear view once more, hung as it were for a few seconds, then she seemed to be caught by some great hand from beneath, and literally hurled into the millrace of the Gut.

"Pretty work," commented Rymer to himself. "But if that Arab bird can do that, I fancy I can. Anyway, I'll either make it before we sink, or I'll pile this old hooker up on Vipeen and fatten the fishes on the sugar."

He teased the sluggish craft along until he could make out the opening of the Gut. He had taken careful note as to just how the native pattimar had gone in, and made up his mind he would follow her tactics, for he figured he could not do better than a man who made the port probably a dozen times a year at all seasons and in all sorts of weather.

He worked his way along about a mile offshore until the narrow width of the Gut was fully visible. Beyond he could see the stretch of the backwater and, of course, now the settlement was plainly visible.

He could see the bungalows of the Europeans at the point known as the Fort, where, four hundred years ago, the Portuguese first landed, and where, later, the Dutch drove them out, only to be evicted in their turn by the British.

Through the Gut he could see the low-lying go-downs at the British trading firms, and an array of masts in the narrow backwater channel, where pattimars lay at anchor. Then they were past the Gut, and Vipeen point hid the inner water from view.

Rymer still kept on until he reckoned he was quarter of a mile or so above the entrance to the Gut. Then he came about, and ran full-and-by until it looked as if he would hit the beach above Vipeen. But he knew what he was doing and, at what he figured was the right moment, he motioned for Mary to take the wheel.

"Hold her just so," he said.

Then he made for the ropes. Down came the mainsail with a rush, and Rymer gathered in the canvas as best he could. But he had little time to spare for that, for he had still the foresail to lower, and then the jib. The canvas plumped on the deck, and dragging it in until he had a free runaway if necessary, he ran back to the wheel. Pushing the girl aside he caught hold of the spokes and jammed the wheel hard over.

The schooner was answering more sluggishly than ever, but gradually she came round, and they drifted down towards Vipeen point, which seemed so close now that they could almost touch it.

They were still travelling under their own impetus to some extent, but it was the down coast current and the inrush of the tide suck that Rymer was "feeling" for, and, just as they seemed on the verge of touching point, he felt it.

It seemed to grip them from beneath. It was like a hand clutching at the keel and pushing it along with an angry impatience.

They swept round the point, and Rymer's brow dripped sweat as he flung the wheel back with all his strength. Years before he had heard of a wicked sandbank which lay just off the opening to the Gut, and he was expecting every moment to hit it.

As a matter of fact, if he had tried to make the Gut direct instead of healing up above and then running down close to the Vipeen shore he would have hit that sandbank. But in following the course of the pattimar, he had done just what he should, and as they were swept into the full rush of the inflowing tide, he heaved a sigh of relief, for he knew he had cleared it.

Now they were full in the Gut, and the wide expanse of the backwater opened up before them. Just on the light, close to the Fort beach, was the Cochin Club, and Mary Trent could see that the Europeans on the tennis courts and the little tenure were all watching the unusual sight of a schooner coming into port with a bareheaded European at the helm. But Rymer saw them not.

The inrush of tide was sweeping full on, so it seemed to him, the Port Office jetty, and he was fighting hard to get her nose round to clear it.

He managed to do so, but then another danger rose as they were swept past the short public jetty, then missing the corner of the coir-yarn pressing wharf by inches, the bowsprit rammed full into one of the picturesque fishing nets, which are only to be seen on the Malabar coast and in China, and which were first brought to Malabar by the Chinese in the twelfth century.

They had not changed a particle in all those centuries, and in appearance are more like some grotesque affair imagined by Heath Robinson than anything else and, one would think, entirely useless for catching fish. But there is nothing more effective in the hands of a Malabar fisherman.

Unchanged in all these centuries! Well, that one was changed, at any rate, for, as the schooner swept past, the bowsprit still caught in the net, there was a ripping and a tearing, and then a terrific crash as the whole box of tricks came down, accompanied by the shrill wailing of the two natives who worked it in partnership.

But Rymer had no time then to spare for that. With the net still clinging to the spar they swept on and raced past long, narrow jetties belonging to different trading firms.

The next danger was the Customs House jetty, but in some miraculous way Rymer got the old hooker past, and then he had to bring the wheel hard a-starboard, for just beyond there the channel swung sharply to the right into the main sweep of the backwater.

And at that the whole front of the native bazaar at Mattancherry loomed up before them. But what was of far more interest to Rymer were the numerous craft which were anchored all along the fairway.

It looked like a perfect, forest of masts and hulks to negotiate, but he clung to the wheel and managed to bring the schooner gradually across until, seizing his chance, he jammed her between two anchored pattimars.

They touched as they swept through, but no damage was done; and then he saw the middle of the backwater, the low-lying mud shoal, known as Vendurthy Island, jammed to the very edge of the water with coco-nut trees.

Rymer headed straight for it. He knew that in against Vendurthy he would find shoal water, and that was what he was seeking. A rickety old steam ferry boat came across just then from the Ernakulam side, but Rymer made them give way, and then, as he saw that he had a chance of making his objective, he motioned urgently for Mary. As she grasped the wheel, he panted:

"Keep her just like she is."

Then he raced forward, and catching hold of one of the anchors, dragged it aft. He swiftly bent on a cable, and he was just in time, for, as he straightened up, the bow of the schooner dug into the mud, and she stopped with a jerk. Then the stern began to swing round slowly, but Rymer was ready and dropped the anchor over the side. He hauled the cable tight, and secured it, and then the motion stopped.

He had made it.

It wasn't a pretty piece of work from a strictly critical point of view; but it was effective, and that was all that mattered just then.

CHAPTER 3. Dr. Huxton Rymer Discovers a Coco-nut Pearl— Plans for the Future.

IT was too late that evening to visit the Port Office, and, as Rymer had his own reasons for not wishing to seek the society of any of the Europeans in the place, neither he nor Mary Trent went ashore. In the absence of any crew it took Rymer all his time to get the schooner shipshape, and Mary took over the galley.

But early the next morning Rymer signalled across to one of the bazaar jetties for a munji, and in this undignified-looking craft he was pulled ashore. He took a rickshaw in the bazaar, and drove through to the Port Office, where he went through the necessary formalities, made a statement as to why he had been forced to seek shelter in that port, and then gave a few necessary particulars regarding the mutiny.

But he did not make any definite charges against the crew, for that would have started the authorities on their trail, and, as long as the survivors were willing to say nothing, Rymer was agreeable.

By this time he was on quite friendly terms with the genial port officer, and when he explained that it would be necessary for him to dispose of his cargo of damaged sugar in Cochin instead of in Bombay, as he had at first intended, the other was all sympathy.

He suggested the names of two bazaar dealers to Rymer, and with this information in his possession Rymer returned in the rickshaw to the bazaar.

He found out which of the two was in the larger way of business, and he decided to visit him first. He had no difficulty in finding his premises, for he occupied fairly extensive godowns on the backwater front.

Rymer entered the place and asked, for Bamjee Haridee, the dealer, in question, but was informed by one of the clerks that his master was then at his coco-nut oil mill, which, Rymer discovered, was some little distance along the backwater at the lower end of the bazaar.

He discovered, too, that he could reach the mill either by boat or by rickshaw, so he resolved to stick to the latter.

He gave the coolie fresh instructions, and away they went through the congested bazaar, through Jewtown—the strange settlement in Mattancherry of white Jews who, so record goes, have been there since the time of Solomon, and who have become so degenerate through centuries of intermarriage that they have been reduced to a mere handful in numbers—and so on until the red, sandy road began to narrow and the bazaar to thin out.

Soon the buildings close to the track disappeared, and Rymer found himself being drawn through the thickly-planted coco-nut trees which are the be-all and end-all of the natives on the Malabar coast.

Another mile or so, and then the coolie drew up. He pointed off to the left, and, through the coco-nut trees, Rymer could see a fairly extensive red-tiled roof with a black iron smokestack rising from it. That, he concluded, must be the mill, so he set off on foot through the trees.

There was a well-defined path which seemed to lead in that direction, and he followed it. The mill was less than a quarter of a mile away, and, as he went along, Rymer noticed little clusters of native huts scattered here and there, and, in front of most of them, women, and children scarcely out of the toddling age, busily engaged in hand-twisting the fibre of the coco-nut husk into the coir yarn of commerce—a product which is familiar enough in England in the form of the so-called "coco mats and matting."

He passed these, and had covered about half the distance from the road to the mill when an incident occurred which, although it seemed trifling enough at the time, was to alter the whole of Rymer's plans just as the unexpected mutiny had brought him into the port of Cochin instead of his making Bombay as he had intended.

Some little distance ahead of his was a coolie, apparently also bound for the mill. In his hand he was carrying a heavy, short; bladed knife something like a Ghurka kukri in appearance. Rymer knew the coast well enough to guess from this that the native was evidently one of the gang employed at the mill for cutting up the coco-nuts, and in this he was right.

His interest in the coolie was no more than that casual thought until, just as the man was passing under a coco-nut tree, one of the nuts in the cluster above suddenly dropped and hit him fair and square on the head.

Now that was not a rare occurrence, as Rymer well knew. And he also knew that; when one of the heavy nuts hit a man bang on the top of the skull it usually dazed him if it didn't knock him senseless for the time being. With children it was a more serious matter, and there are lots and lots of little native youngsters who are killed every year in that way.

On this occasion the thing went quite according to schedule. Bang! It hit the native, and the man, staggering a step or two, fell to the ground. He lay where he had fallen, and Rymer, who had lengthened his stride, was soon bending over him.

It took him just about five seconds to see that the man was unconscious, and, as he straightened up, he saw a native woman and a couple of children running towards him.

He knew it must be the coolie's wife, and that he must live in one of the huts close at hand, so, again bending over him, he took out a pocket-flask of brandy, which he always carried with him in that climate, and forced some of the spirit between the coolie's teeth.

That coolie may have drunk lots of toddy in his day, but he had never had a shot of real old brandy, and the result was just what Rymer hoped. The fellow came round under the urge of the powerful spirit and opened his eyes, spluttering. By this time the woman had thrown herself down beside him, and, seeing that he was more or less all right, looked up at the white man gratefully.

Rymer didn't know much Mallayalaa, but he knew that Hindustani was the lingua franca of the coast, so he spoke to the woman, telling her he was a doctor sahib, and advising her to get her man along home and keep him there for the day.

They got the coolie to his feet, and, supported by the woman and the two children, he went staggering off, only too glad, in fact, to have an excuse for not working.

Then Rymer turned to continue his way to the mill; but, as he did so, his eyes took note for the first time of the nut which had hit the coolie.

He noticed that the impact had broken the husk open, which was certainly odd, for it is no easy matter to open up the outer husk of the coco-nut, even with a knife, for the fibre is most tenacious. However, it had certainly opened in this instance, and it was that which made Rymer bend down and pick up the nut.

He pressed the broken edges apart, and then his head came up with a jerk and his nostrils twitched as a sour, unpleasant smell came from within. He noticed that, instead of being a clean, brown colour and dry, the fibre was of a dirty, green shade, sodden-looking and of a very bad odour. He gazed at it more closely, and then suddenly a faint recollection of a conversation he had once had with a tropical mycologist came to him.

He dropped the coco-nut on the ground, and continued his way to the mill; but all the time his mind was busy trying to recall just what it was the mycologist had said, and, by the time he reached the gates of the mill compound, he had remembered.

On entering the compound he saw great heaps of copra—the meat of the coco-nut— piled on rough stone platforms drying in the sun. All about were coolies with shovels turning the "cups" so that each part would receive the same amount of sun.

Off to one side were other coolies cutting dried "cups" into small pieces, after which they would either be bagged for export in that form or taken into the "chucks" in the mill for crushing on the spot.

Beneath long sheds other coolies were coopering up great Cochin cedar casks, which would later be seasoned before being filled with oil; and then, again, in the shade of other sheds were wet-looking casks already filled with oil ready to be shipped. And here he saw the merchant for whom he was looking.

Bamjee Haridee, one of the richest of the native dealers in the bazaar, was also one of the shrewdest, and, while he undoubtedly had been aware of Rymer's presence the moment he entered the compound, he did not turn until Rymer was close to him.

He was examining the contents of the casks before passing them as fit to be shipped under the rigid clause which reads: "G.P.M.S.D.C.O.F.M.Q.," and which means "Guaranteed Pure Malabar Sun Dried Copra Of Fair Merchantable Quality," was the copra used in crushing, and which the European importers insist on as a condition of purchase.

But he greeted Rymer courteously enough, wondering who this strange European might be, for he knew, of course, that he did not belong to the Cochin commercial community.

Rymer did not state his business there, but waited until the merchant had passed on the last cask for shipment, and then the latter led the way along to a small office at one end of a godown which was right on the shipping jetty. From here either he or the clerk in charge could watch the loading of oil and copra for shipment, or the incoming loads of copra in the native munjis.

He courteously invited his visitor to take a chair, and then called to a boy to bring two young coco-nuts and two glasses. Rymer did not hesitate to accept, for he knew from experience that there is nothing more refreshing than the liquid of a young coco-nut drunk from a freshly-picked nut, and the contents of the one he was given made just a glassful.

He drank it down, and then, looking at the merchant, began to state his business. Bamjee listened in silence to what he had to say, then he raised his shoulders and his hands.

"It is a difficult time for the sugar," he said in quite good English. "Just now my godowns are full and the demand is poor. There has been a lot of Java sugar coming through lately, and the Indian cane crop this year is very large. Besides, yours is damaged."

"Only some of it," Rymer corrected him.

"And all I want you to do is to have a look at it. I know all about the Indian cane crop, and about the Java stuff. I know the market price, too. But you can buy my lot cheap—cheap enough for you to make a good thing out of it. Besides, I have some other business I can put in your way."

The merchant began to show a little more interest.

"That would be, sir?"

"I understand you have a boat-building business, among other things."

"It is only in a small way," deprecated the native. "I build only lighters, which I hire out to the European shipping firms."

"Well, that is enough. I want some repairs done to my schooner. I have mentioned that I had trouble with my crew, and that they left me down the coast. I will tell you more. They mutinied, and I had to drive them over the side. That left me alone to work the schooner into Cochin, and I just made it, for she was leaking badly. I want that leak found and the seams caulked, if you can put your men on the job."

Now Bamjee Haridee knew about that mutiny already. He had not known it had taken place on Rymer's craft until Rymer had said so, but he did know that several strange lascars had landed down the coast, and were even then on their way up the backwater, trying, so his information was, to get a passage in some pattimar for Bombay.

The lascars, however, did not know that Rymer had succeeded in making Cochin in the leaky schooner, but, through the mysterious bazaar telegraph, the merchant had heard the news during the night.

He did not ask the reason of the mutiny. He did not ask anything. It was not his method; nor was it necessary. He could learn all he wanted without showing his hand. So, after pretending to think for some time, he asked Rymer, tentatively, to state a price for his sugar.

Rymer did so promptly. He had already figured over that, since the stuff had cost him no actual cash, he was prepared to sell it for a good deal under the market price. So he named a figure which, he knew, must certainly interest any prospective buyer. They argued back and forth for a bit, and then Bamjee promised to come that afternoon and have a look at the cargo.

That settled, they got down to the question of repairs, and it was not long before he came to terms about a gang to attend to the leak. With this settled, Rymer rose to leave, and, when they had partaken of another green coco-nut, he crossed the compound and started back for the road where the rickshaw was waiting.

On the way, however, he paused long enough to pick up the coco-nut which had struck the coolie on the head an hour or so before, and, on reaching the rickshaw, he tossed it into the bottom. As it was quite an ordinary thing for anyone to pick up a stray coco-nut, the rickshaw coolie paid no attention, or, if he had noticed, he would probably have thought to himself that the sahib was a poor judge of nuts to pick that one. And perhaps Rymer was.

He drove straight back to the jetty where he had landed and secured a munji to put him across to the schooner. It was getting right into mid-morning, the full heat of the day, then, and as he approached the side he found it extremely pleasant to see Mary Trent flitting about the deck, dressed in cool-looking white.

She hailed him gaily as he came over the side, and then Rymer stood still in amazement as he saw a "boy" in clean white just coming out of the galley.

"Where did you get him?" he asked.

"You are not the only one who has been ashore," she answered. "I have just come back. Come along down to the saloon and I will give you a nice cold drink with real ice in it."

Rymer, wondering, followed, and down in the saloon Mary kept her word. She mixed him a long gin sour with a chunk of ice in it, and, as he sipped it gratefully, he waited for her explanation. But, before she gave it, one of the cabin doors opened and a young native boy came out. Rymer waited, and then Mary laughed.

"I went ashore and bought some fresh supplies," she said. "I knew there would be no Europeans at the club at this time of the day, so I drove there first. I got hold of the butler and found him quite willing to be of assistance when I put a ten-rupee note into his hand. The result was twenty-five pounds of ice, a cook and a chokra, and some vegetables which had just arrived from the hills. So I didn't do so badly. Then I went on to the stores and bought some more fresh food. I didn't take any chances on the cook and the chokra, but brought them back with me, and—well, there you are. We haven't any crew, but we can manage with these two boys for the time being."

"I'll say we can," said Rymer with a grin. "My goodness! You are a marvel, Mary!"

"How did things go?" she asked, flushing under his praise.

"I think I will swing them. The port officer is a genial soul, and didn't ask any embarrassing questions. He gave me the names of a couple of bazaar dealers, so I went to see one of them. He shot the same old stuff when I told him I had something to sell, but he is coming here this afternoon to have a look at the stuff. He is also sending a gang under a serang to find the leak and caulk it up. I think he'll buy all right. He stands to make a nice slice of money out of it, and the title to the stuff is good enough, no matter what he may think. This is a straight deal, and we have nothing to fear. But we'll get out of here just as soon as I can. We'll pick up some local men, and make for Bombay and get rid of the schooner there. We ought to clean up half a lakh before we finish. That is no fortune, but it is something to start on, and I guess we will turn it into more."

But Rymer was to change his mind very radically before that day was over. While Mary went back to the deck to give the cook instructions about tiffin, Rymer took his coco-nut along to a spare cabin which he had been using as work-room and chart-room.

He sent the chokra for a hatchet, and then set to work on the nut. It was a messy and smelly business getting through that rotting husk to the nut inside, but Rymer stuck to it until he reached the shell. He found that the hatchet went through this easily, which proved that, like the husk, it was rotting, and, as it came open, an almost overpowering odour rushed forth.

Rymer swore in distaste, but broke the shell apart and opened it up.

The inside was all rotten in appearance. It was just a soft, greenish, pulpy mass, and as he took up one half to examine it, Rymer saw the reason. Now he remembered quite clearly all the mycologist had said to him about coco-nuts, and he knew, from the examination he was making, that he had struck a freak nut just such as that expert had described.

He found all three of the round spots at one end of the nut perfectly hard, which meant that, on maturing, the germ of the nut had sprouted within itself, and had eaten upon its own carcass, so to speak.

It had simply rotted, as the mycologist had said would be the case, when a nut could not find access for its sprout, and now Rymer was all impatience to see if the rest of what the mycologist had said would hold good.

He dug out the sticky mass with his hands until he had got close to the upper end. Then, suddenly, his fingers encountered something hard, and with a grunt, he dragged it out. It came away with a lot of the rotten pulp sticking to it, but he soon wiped this off; and then, as he held the object up, he gave a gasp.

And well he might, for in his hand was glistening what looked to be a perfect pearl.

Rymer took out his handkerchief and polished it. The more he did so the more lustrous did the gem become, and, whatever might be the origin, whatever the mysterious process of Nature which had formed such a lovely jewel in that fetid mess, he knew as sure as he stood there that he was holding one of those rare freaks of which the mycologist had spoken—a coco-nut pearl.

Rymer dragged out a bucket and dumped the whole mess of rotten husk and shell and pulp into it. He put this carefully away, and then, dropping the pearl into his pocket, he opened the door and sent up a loud hail for Mary Trent. She came tripping down the companionway a few seconds later, and he beckoned to her to come into the cabin.

As soon as she had done so, he closed the door and then, taking her across so that they were close to the porthole, he thrust his fingers in the pocket of his khaki shirt.

He took out the pearl and let it roll into the palm of his hand. Then he lifted his hand, opened his fingers, and showed her what was there. She bent over it with a gasp.

"What a beauty!" she whispered, "Where did you get it?"

"You would never believe me if I told you," he answered, in a low tone. "I found it in a strange way, my dear. I'll explain just how to-night. But this is not all. A long time ago I had a talk with a certain man about what has happened to me today. On that occasion, this man—an expert in a certain line—maintained that a certain thing could be done by laboratory means to force Nature to repeat, as often as one wished, a thing that she sometimes produced as a freak. You don't know what I mean, but that will do for now. Well, Mary, I am going to have a shot and see if what he said is a fact. So hold tiffin back until I return. I am going into the bazaar to buy certain things that I shall need in my experiments."

And with that Rymer gave her the pearl to guard and hurried through the saloon.

Rymer was closeted alone in the chart-room most of the afternoon. It was nearly five o'clock when the merchant turned up to have a look at the cargo of sugar, but they could not tell just how many of the bottom layers had been damaged by seawater until they got the whole lot out.

They haggled over the business for an hour or more, but finally came to terms at a figure near what Rymer had set in his own mind, and as it was very much lower than the ruling market price, they were both satisfied.

While Bamjee was there his serang arrived with a gang to have a look for the leak, and when a preliminary examination by one of his divers located it as an opened seam just under the water-line the serang himself went down to feel the extent of it.

It appeared that it was not a very serious matter, but would make it necessary to haul the schooner up at the sheds for the repairs, and it was then arranged that the job should be tackled the next morning, the sugar being unloaded first.

By the following afternoon the cargo was all out, and one of Bamjee's boats towed them along to the shed where the schooner was dragged up on the slip far enough to permit the caulking of the seam.

Rymer and Mary elected to remain on board, for Rymer was keen to proceed with his experiments, and besides, as he worked, he was thinking things over.

Into his mind was coming a great idea which, if his experiments should prove successful, gave promise of being a really big thing. But if he were to proceed with it, he knew that he should need a local ally— a man of considerable influence, and the more he studied the merchant the more convinced was he that Bamjee was the very man he needed as a partner.

By this time, too, Bamjee had sized Rymer up pretty shrewdly, and when, three days later, with the schooner back in the water, her leak caulked and her whole hull glistening with clean white paint, Rymer asked him to come aboard that same evening as he had a business matter to talk over with him, Bamjee knew instinctively that the bearded European might have something to say that would be worth listening to. Whether he took it up or not was a different matter.

So that evening he came out in his little motor-boat to where the schooner lay anchored almost opposite his own mill jetty. Rymer had decided to remain this far down the backwater in order to avoid as much as possible any contact with the Europeans on the station.

For he was dead certain that he had hit on the great secret of which the mycologist had told him, and, if he had, then it would never do to have any of the European commercial community get the breath of a suspicion of what he was up to.

As for Bamjee—well, if they could come to terms, it would be a big thing for both of them. He couldn't go ahead alone; nor could Bamjee. They needed each other, and, to guard against the native double-crossing him, Rymer's protection was to keep the secret of the great scheme inside his own head.

Once again the wonderful pearl was produced as proof of what he had to say. The native acknowledged that he had heard of freak pearls being so produced, but had never actually seen one. But he knew of another merchant in the bazaar who had found one some years before, and had sold it for a very large sum of money to a firm in Bombay.

He was very favourably inclined to listen to what else Rymer had to say when he saw that wonderful pink gem as proof that the other was not romancing, and, late that night, when the fat native stepped into his boat to return to the shore, they had reached an agreement.

It was a fifty-fifty deal between them, and just as soon as Rymer should be in a position to provide certain necessary things, just so soon would Bamjee start going the extensive and intricate machinery which he could command.

So was born one of the greatest plots ever hatched in the East, and the whole thing had had its genesis in a game of dice in Mauritius.

CHAPTER 4.   Tinker Bags a Crocodile—The Journey Back—
The Stranger Aboard "La Sylvide."

TINKER held up a cautioning hand, and shifting his rifle from the left arm to the right, crept along another ten feet or so and flattened himself against the trunk of a coco-nut tree. His companion, a young fellow about his own age, was lying flat on the ground, his tanned young face eagerly strained as he matched Tinker's movements.

Then for a solid five minutes the two remained as motionless as the very trees. Behind them and to the left were the coco-nut trees beneath which the shade was cool and inviting. Immediately on the right was a narrow-sluggish muddy creek which emptied into the backwater a quarter of a mile or so behind them.

On the other side of the creek the coconuts grew just as densely as close at hand, and so still was everything that they might have been two lone crusoes on a desert island for all there was of anyone else to be seen or heard.

But Tinker had spotted a slight movement on the bank opposite him, and he was waiting and watching for it to be repeated. It was not the first time he had been after muggers—crocodiles—and he knew just how wary those giant lizards were. They had left their munji down near the bottom of the creek, and had crept up along the bank as softly as a native could have come. They were clad only in khaki shirts and shorts and topees. Their legs and feet were bare.

And because Tinker was his guest in a way, the other youngster had insisted that Tinker should have first shot at the mugger. They had lain like two shadows waiting for something to show, but so stealthily had the mugger which had caused the ripple across the creek come out of the water and crawled up on to the bank that neither of them had spotted a thing until that moment when Tinker had spied the least little sign.

He knew there was a mugger there somewhere and he was determined to get it.

Peering across, he could see nothing. Had the bank been more open he might have made out the grey dead-looking form that would seem so much like a log; but the grass grew fairly long just there, and, if Mr. Mugger was on the bank it was concealing him.

Still they waited. They were both pretty well seasoned *shikaris*, but Tinker had done a considerable amount of hunting all over the globe, while the youngster who was with him had been born in India and had bagged his first panther when only twelve and his tiger when he was sixteen.

And just as they hoped, the mugger presently decided to come across the creek where there was a little patch of sunlight in which he could drowse. He slipped into the water like an evil grey shadow, and then from either side came the tell-tale ripples as he swam across.

Tinker did not shoot. The mugger was making straight for the side on which he stood, and if he kept quite still there was a chance that he would get a much better shot. If the reptile should change its mind and go up or down stream, he would risk a water shot, but he wasn't keen on it, for the mugger would probably go under whether hit or not; and then there would be the dickens of a mess trying to get him up. Which simply goes to show that Tinker knew his game.

But the mugger was quite definitely bound for that sunny patch on the bank about a dozen yards from where Tinker stood flattened against the tree. The tip of the wedge-like nose came nearer and nearer, and then, risking a slow, slow twist of the head, Tinker saw the whole snout appear from the water. Next, the repulsive armoured neck and back followed, and the creature—a big fourteen-foot brute if he was an inch—waddled up the bank, turned round leisurely, so that he was facing the water, in readiness to slide in like a wraith at the first hint of danger, and flattened himself in the mud.

Tinker scarcely breathed. He wiggled a toe at his companion to signal that he had the mugger placed, and then he began to get ready to shoot. It was quite an interesting display of just how slowly a human being can work well-controlled muscles to see Tinker come into action.

There was none of the exaggerated lift of the slow-motion film in the lad's movements. He was like a well-oiled machine, and the eyes of his companion glistened in approval as he watched.

Tinker worked his gun fraction of an inch by fraction of an inch around the swelling bole of the palm. Now he had the ridged trunk between him and the mugger, and with this cover he got his rifle at the cock. Then slid on round the trunk until he could just see the snout. He brought up his rifle with infinite caution, and levelled it.

He stood then, quite motionless, watching that snout for the slightest sign of movement. But the mugger was unsuspicious so far, and Tinker completed his motion He shifted his shoulder out inch by inch until, on looking again, he could see one eye of the mugger.

He brought his cheek down until it was nestling against the butt; his left eye closed, and his right sought along the barrel. His finger rested lightly on the trigger, and then, at the very moment when he had a bead on that eye, he pressed the trigger.

The silence of the jungle was shattered as the heavy .405 crashed out, and, on the very echo of the crash, Tinker's companion came to his feet. Tinker was out from behind the tree like a flash, and the pair rushed ahead where the crocodile was tearing up the place in a death frenzy.

He was half in and half out of the water by the time they reached him, and even in that last terrific convulsion which sent them back, his great jaws snapped like a giant steel trap.

Then some instinct away inside him made him try one last time to get under water, but by this both Tinker and his companion had the brute by the tail, and were hanging on like grim death.

The tail flailed back and forth, but they stuck to it; and then they managed to get hold of one hind flipper, if it might be so-called. And that did the trick. They dragged the carcase back on to the bank and stood back to make sure that those wicked jaws were really harmless.

And as they saw the eye where Tinker's bullet had entered as true as could be, they knew the old brute would never snap another piccaninny.

It was a fine bit of work, and it is little wonder that Tinker was pleased with himself. Nor did his companion stint his praise.

"It was a poach of a shot," be exclaimed. "You are some lad on the trigger, Tinker, I'll tell you. That old brute must be fourteen feet if he is an inch, and his teeth will be worth keeping. Why don't you keep the hide as well? We can send a couple of coolies over to skin him!"

"I was thinking that is what I shall do, Jack," answered Tinker, as he saw the extent of the hide. "I could get a fairish size bag out of that skin if I could get it tanned properly."

"Easiest thing in the world," said his companion enthusiastically. "We can get it skinned and stick it in salt in an empty kerosene oil tin. Then we can seal that up and send it up north to the Cawnpore tannery. They will turn it out in six months as fine a job as you can get done anywhere. And then I know a firm over in Madras who will make it into whatever you wish. You leave it to me. I'll attend to it for you and send it on to England to you when it is finished."

"I believe I will do just what you say, but with one difference," said Tinker. "I'll send it up to the Cawnpore Tannery, but you must have it made up in Madras into a bag or whatever you wish. You gave me first shot at him, so it is only fair you should share the spoils."

Jack didn't see why he should agree to this, and so a good-natured quarrel began which ended in Tinker getting his way. So, knowing it would be useless to look for more mugger in that little creek just then, they turned their steps back.

They had covered some twenty yards or so, and Jack McGregor, Tinker's friend, was in the lead, when all of a sudden Tinker heard him give a yell, and the next instant he dropped his rifle and threw himself forward. Tinker jumped to one side to see what was up, and then his eyes goggled as he saw Jack struggling with what his startled gaze told him was nothing else than a young mugger.

He dashed in to help, and between them they got the young devil's front flippers drawn back behind it, thus rendering it helpless, so that they could hold it and keep away from its teeth. But from these there was no real danger, for the croc was still too young to do any damage.

"Nearly three feet," remarked Jack. "If I only had a place in the compound I'd take him along and keep him. Might ship him home to some zoo and make a bit of money out of him. But I guess he would be more bother than he would be worth. What do you say, Tinker? Shall we let him go again?"

Tinker looked at the little monster, now so harmless, but soon to become another vicious brute to prey on native dogs and pigs and children such as he had shot. Then his eyes began to twinkle, and he turned to Jack.

"I've got a peach of an idea," he said. "Listen, Jack. If it comes off we ought to get quite a lot of fun out of it. If it doesn't, well, we can push the little brute back into the water and let him go. What do you think of this?"

Then he began to talk, and as he proceeded Jack broke into chuckles. When Tinker had finished he laughed outright.

"If it only works," he said. "Old Brosher is in the very same place every evening. It's worth trying if we can get in there without being seen. If your guv'nor catches us he will skin us alive, but if you are game to risk it, I am."

"I'm game all right," responded Tinker.

"We can tie him up with that coil of coir rope we left in the munji. Give me a hold, and I'll help you carry him down."

So, despite the struggles of the young mugger they lugged him along with them and dumped him into the bottom of the munji, where they secured him with some or the coir rope they had brought along with them. Then they stowed their rifles away carefully and got in, each taking a paddle, for the four-mile journey across the backwater to Cochin whence they had started out on their shooting expedition.

It was getting along late afternoon then, and the sun was already sinking low in the west. The great ball could just be seen above the palms on the other side of the backwater, and already the red roofs of the buildings in the bazaar were in cool shadow. They headed straight for the opposite shore in order to get away from the main channel current and then turned up there, paddling in close by the bazaar jetties, which course would bring them eventually up round the turn of the channel, past the customs-house jetty, and then along by the jetties belonging to the European firms. From there it was only a short paddle to the beach in front of the club which was their objective.

As they went along, Jack, whose father was manager of one of the commercial firms, and who lived in the place, pointed out interesting bits of the bazaar from time to time, giving Tinker stray slices of history or legend, which boys pick up in the most mysterious way, and which are often far more interesting and authentic than that gathered by the grown-ups.

Then, after a little silence, he lifted his arm and pointed to a small white schooner which rode at anchor just opposite a big range of red-tiled buildings.

"I'd like to go up the coast, or out to the Laccadives in that," he said. "She looks like a speedy little thing, and clean, which is what a pattimar isn't."

"You don't often see anything like that in here I should think," remarked Tinker. "She is the first I have spotted down this way."

"Yes. And she is owned by a European, too. That is a rare thing to see here. I don't know anything about him, except I heard dad say he had been driven in here by the schooner springing a leak. He had a cargo of sugar, and sold it in the bazaar. Dad says he almost gave it away."

"A European, eh?" remarked Tinker. "That is unusual, isn't it? Does he come to the club?"

"No; I fancy he isn't the club sort. Then he has his wife with him—or a woman, anyway. I have seen her in a rickshaw. She's a peach, I can tell you, and dresses mighty well. But they don't come to the club."

"That's kinda queer in a place like this," said Tinker. "Let's paddle along closer to her, and give her the once-over, Jack."

"All right; we can go past on the other side of her."

They shifted their course a little, and sent the munji along in the new direction. The schooner which had attracted their attention was then only a couple of hundred yards distant, and, as they drew nearer, Tinker could make out her name.

"La Sylvide, Mauritius," he read, and then he noticed that someone was leaning over the stern rail. They paddled on, heading the munji so they would pass on the starboard side of the schooner, and as they came along it was evident that the person leaning over the stern rail was watching them.

Presently Tinker saw that it was a woman, dressed in white, and just then she was joined by a big man, garbed in a silk suit. He wore a beard, and, now that the sun was low, had discarded his topee. He turned round to look towards them, for apparently the woman had said something to him.

Then Tinker could see that he wore a pointed black beard, and, as the munji got still nearer, there seemed something vaguely familiar about the man.

They shot another ten yards ahead, and then Tinker, who was in the stern, brought his paddle round so as to clear the stern anchor-line. He and Jack had also discarded their topees, and, as he lifted his head once more, the westering sun shone full upon him.

And it was in that moment his eyes rested full on those of the woman, and then on those of the man. To say that he was startled was to put it mildly. The dead mugger back in the creek had received no worse a shock when Tinker's bullet plunged into his eye than Tinker, relatively speaking, did in that moment.

For his startled gaze had recognised, first Mary Trent, and then Dr. Huxton Rymer.

The next second the munji shot round the stern of the schooner, and they were sliding past. He said nothing of his discovery to Jack, but as they paddled on he knew that both Mary Trent and Rymer had recognised him.

CHAPTER 5. Tinker's Practical Joke—The Station in an Uproar—A Surprise for Sexton Blake.

IT was dusk when Tinker and Jack drove the munji on to the beach in front of the club. Out through the Gut, they could see just a faint line of pink against the western horizon of the sea, but back in the east the heavy curtain of night was already being drawn down, hiding the distant ranges from view.

The grotesque fishing-nets had been drawn up for the night, and were hanging slack against the crazy frames. The palms looked lonely and drear, but, against the western sky, sharply cut in plumy silhouette. The kites and the crows were gone, but the flying foxes were sweeping high overhead.

The pattimars swung silent in the channel anchorage, over Vipeen way a native was singing in a high-pitched voice, from the bazaar came the faint thrum-thrum of a tom-tom being beaten monotonously. The Fort was finishing its day; the bazaar was just waking up.

Tinker and Jack dragged the munji out of reach of the tide, and stole up the sandy beach until they were close to the wall of the club. The building was originally an old go-down, flanking right on the edge of the beach, and, by rising on tiptoe, they could peer through the windows, which were open.

At the eastern end was the ladies' room, seldom occupied at that hour of the evening. Then came a small concrete terrace, newly built, which connected the ladies' room, or "dovecot," as it was more commonly known, with the main building. At that end was a reading-room, then came the billiard-room, and, finally, the bar. Next were the kitchens, and a short distance away the new club chambers. It was not a very extensive club, for Cochin is a small station.

On such a cool evening, and at that hour, Tinker and Jack had counted on most of the members still being in the chairs by the tennis-courts, or on the terrace, for it was only in the monsoon or on a sweltering night that they reluctantly sought the interior for shelter, or the punkahs, as the case might be, and as they crossed the strip of beach they could hear voices on the terrace.

They kept on until they reached one of the open windows which gave on to the bar, and there the two plotters crouched down to listen. They waited a minute or so, but no sound of voices came to them.

Then they risked peering in, and the moment their eyes were over the edge of the sill they drew back hastily and clutched each other in a paroxysm of pure joy, for the quarry they had been seeking was exactly where they had hoped to find him.

Even as they crouched down again, they heard a thick voice raised. It said:

"Boy!"

There was a mumble as the bar-boy answered, and then the "slush" of feet on matting, as the boy crossed the bar. Next they heard the "pop!" of a cork, and after that the "s-s-zz!" of an opened soda-water bottle. Came the splash of water in a glass.

Again they risked a peep in, and now they remained longer. In one of the low club chairs, just inside the window, was a very stout man, dressed in white. He was sprawled out in the chair, with a glass of whisky-and-soda in his right hand and a half-smoked cigar in his left. The side of his face which was visible was of a mottled purple shade, and he was wheezing like an old cab-horse as he breathed heavily. The bar-boy had gone back to his place behind the bar, and was already dozing off again.

There wasn't another soul in the place, but just then they heard the click of balls in the billiard-room, and Tinker touched Jack's arm, while he went along to the next window, to peer in.

He came back, and held up one finger, which meant that there was a solitary member in there, knocking the balls about by himself. And then Tinker made a suggestive movement of the head towards the munji, which meant that they had better get busy.

Now, those two young rascals had decided back on the bank of the creek what they would do if conditions were favourable, and they had found them almost better than they had dared hope.

The fat man in the bar was the very quarry they had been looking for, and each youngster knew only too well that he was notorious as the station toper.

Over on the Madras side, when a member of the Madras club tries to be facetious in the presence of a Cochin man, he usually says: "Cochin? Oh, yes, I have heard of Cochin! Let me see, it is an island, isn't it, entirely surrounded by whiskies-and-sodas?" Which, it may be remarked, gets the hard-working Cochin man peeved at times. But it was a pretty rapid place in the old days, and the old toper on whom Tinker and Jack had designs was a relic of those times.

They didn't know just what quantity he actually drank, but it was commonly said that he hadn't drawn a sober breath for twenty-four years, and it was a mystery to everyone how he escaped having delirium tremens.

Well, with everything apparently set just as they would wish, Tinker and Jack went back to the munji and dragged out the young mugger they had captured on the bank of the creek. The little brute was as active as a wild cat, and fought bad to wriggle clear; but they held him securely and carried him back across the beach until they were again under one of the bar windows.

Tinker took another look inside. The fat man had gulped some more of his drink, and was gazing in a bleared fashion at the palm-thatched roof of the building. Behind the bar the "boy" was sound asleep. From the billiard-room Tinker could still hear the click of billiard balls coming over the low partition. Still no one else was in view.

He dropped back and made a sign. He caught hold of the mugger and held his legs twisted back while Jack slipped off the noose. Then they heaved the struggling reptile up, and booted him over the window-sill into the bar.

There was a flop as he went over, and at first they dodged back to run. But as nothing happened they risked peeping in again, and now they saw that the young mugger, evidently puzzled by the strange place into which it had dropped, was lying just about half way between the window and the chair where the fat toper sat.

Even as they watched, it began creeping along in that direction, and then it paused close to the man's leg. It seemed to nose into him in an inquiring way and, at the touch, the toper brought his gaze back from the ceiling and looked down.

Tinker and Jack saw an expression of dumbfounded amazement enter his eyes as he saw the slimy reptile at his feet. Then this was succeeded by a goggling look of sheer horror, and the next second the glass crashed to the floor as he let out a terrific yell, and came to his feet.

"My heavens! Oh, my heavens! I've got them at last!" he yelled. Then he turned, and as the mugger started for him, he tried to jump both chair and table which lay between him and safety. The table went over with a crash. The boy behind the bar had already started up at his yell, and he saw the fat man streaking across towards the door with a mugger flopping about like a crazy thing, half scared to death at the rumpus and snapping viciously, he disappeared like a flash through the door leading to the kitchen.

The fat man disappeared in the direction of the compound, and no sooner was he gone than the member, who had been knocking the balls about on the billiard table, pushed open the swing door to see what was the cause of the uproar. Coming straight towards him, it seemed, was the biggest crocodile he had ever seen, and that one look was enough. He let go the door and made for the other end of the club, squeaking like a scared rabbit as he went.

Tinker and Jack saw no more of the proceedings just then, for they had fallen from the sill in convulsions of joy, and were rolling over and over on the sand in a frenzy of glee. But there were others who found themselves taking an unwilling part in the upheaval started by the two young imps.

The tennis had finished at dusk, and the players, with warm jerseys thrown about their shoulders, were idling on the sitting-out place near the nets, talking and sipping cool drinks. In the group there were three ladies— a rather stout matron, who had been on the station for some years, a girl—the only unmarried one in the place, and a young woman, who had come out from home newly married.

For men, there were three who had been playing tennis, and had not yet gone on home to change. There was also Mr. Sexton Blake, who was visiting on the station, and there was, lastly, a tall, long-limbed young man who, just then, was leaning over the back of the unmarried young girl's chair entertaining her with his many feats of prowess during the late war.

He was in the act of detailing some of his stirring experiences while flying—as a matter of fact, he had never been up in his life—when, from the direction of the club, there came the sound of a soul in mortal distress, and a few moments later, out of the dusk there appeared what looked at first like a young elephant on the rampage.

It was the fat toper hoofing it along at a terrific pace, and so crazed was he with what he thought was an attack of delirium tremens, that he did not even see the group by the nets. He thudded by, his eyes goggling and wild words bursting from his lips. Then, while the whole group stared in stupefaction at the sight, he was again swallowed by the dusk. They were still staring at each other when there came another yell, and once more a white-clad figure came plunging out of the shadows. It went past like a streak, and the group had just time to recognise it as one of the staidest members of the club when he too disappeared in the direction of the *maidan*.

On top of this a perfect hullabaloo broke out near the kitchen quarters and the chambers, and there was the sound of excited voices trailing down towards the other gate, which led to the main road. The bar boy's panic had been taken up by the other servants, and they were one and all in flight.

Sexton Blake and the three tennis players rose, intending to go into the club and try to find out what was wrong. But, even as they turned, they stood transfixed as something came up the gravelled path full at them.

From her chair the fat lady gave a terrified squeal and rose. The young man, who had been leaning negligently over the pretty girl's chair, suddenly found most urgent business to attend to, and disappeared in the wake of the fat man and the billiard idler. The stout lady had started to run like a scared rabbit, and had fetched up full against the coarse coir back nets of the tennis courts, where she was clawing away frantically as if trying to climb to high heaven.

The young matron was on her chair, with her skirts pulled tight about her ankles. The pretty girl had taken one look, and had flopped back in hysterics, and then she yelped to a wild scream, as what she took to be some unbelievably ferocious monster of the sea came plunging on into the circle of light.

Sexton Blake had seen at first glance that it was a mugger, and his second glance told him it was very young, and probably not dangerous. Two of the tennis players saw the same thing, while the third was not so certain, but stood his ground.

Then, as the reptile flopped to the right and seemed to make straight for the terrified stout lady, who was still clawing at the back netting, Blake made a dive for the mugger and missed it by about an inch.

One of the other young men was plucky enough to grab at it, but he too missed, and then he and Blake collided with force as Blake threw himself forward once more. They bounced back from each other, and Blake jumped forward. This time he succeeded in getting his hands on the little brute. He was forced to fall flat to the ground to hang on, but he managed to do so before the reptile reached the fat lady, and after a few moments' struggle he got hold of the mugger's flappers, and dragged them back in the way which held the brute quite helpless.

At that moment there sounded more footsteps coming up the path at a run, and the next second Tinker and young Jack McGregor came within the penumbra of light. They saw Blake struggling with the mugger, and without any hesitation hastened forward to give him a hand.

Their bravery made considerable impression on the pretty girl and the young matron, who were both quite interested in the proceedings and admired the way the famous detective had acted. But Blake did not share their feelings. No sooner did he see the pair of young imps, and note the twitching of their lips, than he knew he needed to look no farther for the authors of the outrage.

He said nothing, but permitted them to help him lift up the mugger and carry it off. He led the way down the path to the lower end of the club, and then, when they were out of earshot, he said grimly: "Which way did you bring it?"

Tinker motioned towards the beach; he could not speak. Blake led the way through the bar, and stood by while they lifted the mugger out.

He hopped out after them, and ordered them to set it free. Then, while the pair were in the act of turning to resume their enjoyment of the joke, Blake caught each by the collar, and before they knew what he was up to, he had flopped them down hard upon the sand.

He held Tinker while he rubbed Jack's head and face into the sand, forcing the grit between his teeth and almost choking him. Then he turned his attention to Tinker, and gave him a worse doing than he had Jack, for, as he muttered savagely while he did so:

"I'll wager it originated with you, you young scamp, so you get the worst of it. I'll teach you to scare people by turning muggers loose in the club compound."

But even Blake was forced to desist after a while, and when he released them, the pair staggered back down the beach to see if the mugger had taken to the water, and then they hung on to each other, quaking with helpless glee at the recollection of the fat man tearing off in a frenzy of fear, thinking that at last Nemesis had come upon him.

Blake left them there and vaulted through the window. As he emerged from the bar he saw a group of the club "boys" standing down near the gates, so he went along and scolded them, sending them back to their work. Then he walked along to the other end, where he found that the ladies had recovered somewhat, and were relating their experience to two new arrivals.

At that moment the long-limbed young man, who had found urgent business to attend to when he had deserted the pretty girl, came up, panting, and, with the coolest effrontery in the world, said:

"Well, I caught up with him. He is in a terrible state. He thinks he has the d.t.'s. But I told him it was all right."

The pretty girl's lip curled, and she looked across at Blake. The two of them suddenly smiled in understanding, and even the bounce of that blowhard could not stand up under their unspoken scorn. He hummed and hawed for a bit, and then, seeing that the girl had "got his number," as the saying goes, he slipped away in the shadows and made for the bar.

At that moment Blake's host, an engineer who was visiting the station on a special mission, and whom Blake had come to Cochin to see, drove up in a rickshaw. Blake at once prepared to get his own rickshaw to go along to the other's bungalow, and was in the act of getting in when Tinker came along and touched him on the arm.

"I say, guv'nor, let's walk across," he said. "I've got something to tell you."

Blake looked at him suspiciously, but saw that Tinker was quite serious now, so, as the bungalow at which they were staying was only across the maidan, he consented. He called to Bailey, the engineer, telling him they would walk; then he and Tinker waved a good-night to those who still remained, and started down the drive.

Tinker waited until they had reached the road where they could not be overheard by any coolies, then he turned to Blake and said:

"There is a schooner anchored down the backwater, guv'nor. Jack and I passed it on our way back this afternoon. And whom do you think I saw leaning over the rail?"

"I can't imagine, my lad. Is this what you wanted to tell me? Whom did you see?"

"Dr. Huxton Rymer and Mary Trent, guv'nor."

"Rymer! And Mary Trent! Are you positive, my lad?"

"Absolutely, sir! And what's more, I am certain they recognised me, too. What do you suppose they are doing, guv'nor?"

"I have no idea, Tinker. Rymer and Mary Trent in a schooner

anchored down the backwater! It seems distinctly odd. If we get a chance we shall try and find out what the schooner is doing there."

At that Blake left it for the time being. But, as they walked along, his mind was very busy wondering just what the pair would be doing in Cochin, for he and Tinker had been on the station for three days, and he had neither heard nor seen anything of Rymer.

And here it may be as well to explain just, how Blake and Tinker happened to be there.

CHAPTER 6.   The Coco-nut Disease—The Missing Mycologist—Blake's Experiments.

SEXTON BLAKE and Tinker were in Madras when Blake received a cablegram from England which caused him to alter his plans at the last moment. He had come out to India on behalf of a certain rajah in order to investigate certain financial matters for that gentleman, and had brought his mission to a successful close.

In Madras he had found those who were actually behind a gigantic swindle of which the rajah was the victim, and, after a short but strenuous session with them, Blake had forced them to disgorge the bulk of their ill-gotten gains. He and Tinker were staying at the Madras Club as guests of "Big Tim" Congrove, the chief of the C.I.D. in Madras, and had booked passages by one of the City Line boats which was due to leave that port for home two days after Blake received the cable which caused him to alter his intention.

This cable was from the managing director of a very large soap-making firm in England. It was a company in which Sexton Blake was a fairly extensive shareholder, and on more than one occasion in the past he had attended to certain matters for the company. Just how the managing director, Lord Bandon, knew he was in Madras he didn't know, unless his worthy housekeeper, Mrs. Bardell, had given that gentleman the information.

At any rate, the cable had reached him, having been sent direct in care of the Bank of India, and the gist of it was that Lord Bandon was anxious for Blake to go across to the Malabar Coast before proceeding to England, and there make a thorough investigation of the copra and coconut oil question on behalf of the soap company.

The cable further advised Blake that the company already had an engineer on the spot looking into the technical side of the matter, for, the cable explained, the company was considering the advisability of erecting a thoroughly up-to-date coconut oil mill on that coast.

What they particularly wanted from Blake was a report on the average annual output of copra and oil, the present area under trees, and what the chances of increase or diminution of crop were for some years to come. Also just what system of purchasing for the mill would be necessary, and how their coming to the coast would affect other dealers and crushers. Then, of course, any other details that might arise.

From a personal point of view, the mission would have been a welcome one to Blake, for it was different from the usual run of cases which he usually had in hand, and he was very fond of anything along business or financial lines.

Still, he was already finding that he should be on his way to England, and, if it had not been on behalf of a company in which he himself was heavily interested, he would have been inclined to refuse.

However, the upshot was he cabled back to Lord Bandon that he would run across to Malabar and see what he could find out, so, on the very same day, he telegraphed to Bailey, the engineer who was investigating the technical side of the matter, that he was coming.

On reaching Ernakulam, the railway terminus on the land side of the backwater, they did not find the engineer waiting; but he had sent a motor-boat to meet them, and a letter, saying they would find rickshaws waiting for them at the public jetty in Cochin, and to drive right on to the bungalow which had been lent him while he was there. He explained that he had to go down the backwater to look at a mill site, but would join them before dinner.

That was three days before the incident, at the club in which Tinker and young Jack McGregor had played leading roles, and during that time Blake had been busily employed looking into the matter which had brought him there, while Tinker played about more or less.

And in that three days, what with his own poking about the topes and the bazaar, and his conversations with various Europeans and natives, Blake had gathered a good deal of valuable information.

But one thing which stood out from everything else was the somewhat startling fact that, if the production of coconuts should continue as at present, that industry, which was the whole life of the coast, would soon disappear. And the puzzling thing was that the threat of this had only arisen recently.

It came to Blake from a dozen different sources, and boiled down to this:

Up to three months before the crop of nuts had been quite normal, and even extending. For some years past the Europeans had been trying to drive it into the heads of the natives that they could secure a larger crop, and extend the life of their trees from ten to twenty-five years, if they would but adopt the system of wide planting instead of smothering their trees in close together.

This idea was gaining ground, as actual proof had been shown them, and, should it proceed, the output of nuts, which meant more copra—hence more coco-nut oil and more coir yarn, was inevitable.

But about three months before the nuts, for a distance of some six miles above and below Cochin, had been attacked by a strange disease which threatened to wipe out the industry in that part altogether.

And as it was just there that the soap company was planning to erect its mill, the point which Blake had to decide was whether it was a condition which would pass, or was it of such a nature that the trees would never recover.

The curious part was that the trees themselves seemed healthy enough, and, moreover, those nuts which were marketable appeared just as sound as ever. But in each tope a very large percentage of the young nuts seemed to become attacked by a mysterious disease, which not only ruined the meat of the nut for seed or copra purposes, but rotted the fibre as well, which, of course, made it unsuitable for coir yarn.

The European merchants were no end worried over this development. The first thing they had done was to seek the services of a fully qualified mycologist, and for some time past a young man had been at work studying the trees, and trying to solve the mystery.

In the bazaar the native merchants had joined with the Europeans, and the Cochin State Government, in conjunction with the Travancore Government, had contributed a large sum of money for the purpose.

But so far the mystery was as deep as ever. That it was a reality could be no doubt, for Blake had secured some of the rotten nuts himself, and, on the very evening on which the mugger incident at the club had occurred, he had completed a very careful examination of several of them. And in that he had made a most startling discovery which he was keeping to himself.

It was a discovery which the young mycologist should have made himself, had it not been that he was, in Blake's opinion, working from the wrong end of the question. He had taken it for granted that the disease was one which had its genesis in the roots or the trunk; whereas, Blake had begun his analysis with the nut itself.

He had been undecided whether to tell Bailey about it that night after dinner, or to proceed along the same lines for a day or two longer before saying anything. In this his decision was influenced by something which the engineer told him when they had finished dinner, and were sitting under the punkahs on the veranda, smoking.

"I heard some rather disturbing news to-day," announced the engineer, when the boy had taken his departure. "Did you see Craven or Phillips at the club?" (These were two of the leading Europeans on the station).

Blake shook his head.

"No. I was busy in the back room here until it was too late for tennis. I changed and went across just about half an hour before you showed up. There were not many there to-night. What is the thing of which you speak?"

"It is about Green, the mycologist, who has been working round about the place for the last couple of weeks. There is nothing definite, but he seems to have disappeared.

"Disappeared? I don't quite understand. Do you mean he is lost?"

"Well, I don't see how that is possible. I will tell you all I know. It seems that the day before yesterday he told Phillips (he has been staying at his bungalow, you know) that he was going across the back-water and start to work on some of the trees over there. The spot he referred to was one just about opposite Vendurthy Island, and, putting it at the limit he would cover, he couldn't, at any time, have got more than ten miles distant from Cochin, unless he changed his mind after he left.

"He was to be back last evening in order to see the Travancore mycologist who was passing through on his way to Madras. It was important that he should have done so, for the question of this disease which has attacked the trees is to be taken up with the Madras Government. Well, Green didn't turn up—neither during the evening nor the night.

"He didn't have much food with him— had taken just enough to last him about a day. Nor did he have a boy. Phillips' motor-boat had set him ashore near the spot where he intended working, and it went to the same place last evening to pick him up. It waited all night, but he didn't appear. The serang came back this morning to report to Phillips, and he decided to wait until this evening. He sent the boat back to wait, but up to five o'clock Green hadn't come.

"Then Phillips began to get a bit worried. I met him down the backwater—he had gone himself to see if he could find Green. He had put a gang of men, under one of his young assistants, into the tope to scour the land thoroughly to see if they could find Green. I met him on the road just before I came to the club, and he said they still had no news. He and Craven were talking of having a general turn-out of all Europeans, and I thought they may have come on to the club to spread the news.

"It is rather puzzling what could have happened. I don't see how Green can be lost, for the coco-nut belt there extends in land for four or five miles, and it is all open tope. No chance to get lost as in the jungle. And there is no dangerous game in there, either. It is my opinion he must have gone off down the backwater on something that came up after he left Phillips' bungalow. He will probably turn up to-night. It would be easy enough for him to get food from any of the native huts as he went along."

Blake nodded thoughtfully.

"You may be right," he said at last. "Tinker was over that way shooting muggers to-day. Did you see any signs of another European, Tinker?"

"Not a soul, guv'nor. We went about a quarter of a mile or so up a small creek there. It was just about opposite Vendurthy Island. But didn't see or hear a sound of anyone."

Blake turned back to Bailey; then he rose.

"Excuse me a moment," he said. "I have something rather interesting to-show you. And, in the meantime, can you make quite sure that none of your servants will overhear what I have to say?"

Bailey, wondering, nodded that he would do so, and Blake made for the back room where he had been carrying out his experiments. He rummaged about there in the bottom of the big box in which he had placed the rotten refuse of the nuts and husks, and then he started back to the veranda, his hand closed tightly over something which he had taken from the box.

Bailey came back at the same moment, and Blake motioned for both him and Tinker to come close to the light. Then he opened his hand, and, at sight of what he held, they gave vent to a gasp of sheer amazement.

CHAPTER 7. The Connection of the Schooner—The Melba— The Diseased Nuts and the Missing Mycologist—The Detective Expounds a Theory.

"PEARLS!"

Bailey shot out the exclamation in a whisper, and Tinker echoed it with a nod. Blake smiled a little as he gazed down at the three irregular spheres which gleamed iridescently beneath the white light of the petrol gas-lamp which stood on the table.

"Yes," he said, as he closed his fingers and slipped the three pearls into his pocket.

"At least, that is how they would be classified on any pearl market; but it is seldom indeed that this particular type of pearl is found."

The engineer looked at him blankly.

"I don't understand," he said. "I have never heard of pearl oysters being found in this part of the world, although I know there are fisheries in Ceylon and a fairly large market for the Persian Gulf pearls at Bombay."

"Sit down, both of you," said Blake. "I will tell you something that may surprise you." Then, when they were seated, he went on:

"You are quite right, Bailey. Nor have I ever heard of pearl oysters in these waters. But that doesn't matter. These specimens did not come out of pearl oysters."

"Not out of pearl oysters? You have me guessing, Blake."

"Listen! You have been so wrapped, up in your profession, Bailey, that you have not had time to learn very much about the coconut. You came here to pick out a site for an oil mill, and you have confined yourself to that. But I am here to look into the question from a different angle, and in that I have to consider the proposition from the point of view of supply and demand of copra for your mill.

"Well, this isn't the first time I have had to deal with the coconut, and I can assure you I have always found it a most engrossing study. The last time I was engaged on a case in connection with the nut, I took the trouble to make a fairly comprehensive study of it—the various forms of cultivation, and so on. At that time I talked with many men and gathered many interesting facts. For instance, I am willing to wager you cannot tell me how many different types of coir yarn are manufactured from the soaked and beaten fibre which is got

45

from the husk."

"No, I don't know."

"Well, there are more than seventy types twisted and shipped from this coast. It ranges in thickness from a fine string, so to speak, to a rope yarn, and is used all over the world for many, many purposes. At home you can see it in the ordinary coco-mats and mattings of commerce, to the nose-bags with which nearly every dray-horse in London is provided; in the Straits, and on the China Coast, it is used in the form of rope. In Australia and South Africa, you see it in the form of dyed matting for cricket pitches. And in the United States and Canada, it is employed in numerous ways, from the making of mats to the twisting of giant rope-nets which are the basis of the mud dykes on the famous levees of the Mississippi River. And if you take the trouble to look out of the train windows as you pass through Kent, in England, you will see it used in the miles and miles of supports for the hop vines.

"But that is en passant. What I want to get at is that there is a lot about the coco-nut that is not generally known, and one of them is a thing so rare that lots of mycologists have no knowledge of it. Now, this is what I mean."

Then Blake began, and gave a brief but full dissertation on the peculiarity of the nut when the three holes in the end are blocked by some freak of Nature. He explained just how the rare coco-nut pearl is formed by the inner shoot growing back upon itself, and stated one or two instances when the resulting pearl had been found. In this way, he led them up to what he had shown them a few minutes before.

"Those three pearls which I showed you are coco-nut pearls," he said. "I found them myself this afternoon, so there can be no doubt about it. They are beautiful specimens—at least, two of them are, and will command a high price in any market. And this brings me to the result of my investigations so far.

"You know why I am here, Bailey. You know, too, what everyone on the coast is puzzled over—the strange disease which appears to have attacked so many of the trees, and which is spreading up and down the backwater. Now, I haven't the slightest doubt that Green would have hit what I have hit sooner, only he had been attacking the problem from the other end. Now, I have explained to you that this particular disease is of very rare occurrence. It isn't a disease really—just a freak of Nature.

46

"But all the nuts which I have examined arc diseased, which is proof that the trouble is not due to that freak. That was the problem I had to solve. I went through a large number of nuts—more than a hundred. In only three of them did I find pearls, but, even at that, it is a high percentage, more so than in oyster pearling.

"The question then was: How did this disease start so suddenly? I could not find the trees affected. Nuts taken from the same cluster were perfectly healthy and sound. So how could it have come about?

"That was when I redoubled my efforts. I took quite immature nuts and gave them the most minute examination. Not a single particle of the surface did I allow to escape the magnifying glass. And early this afternoon I began to suspect that I had found something. It was this:

"In one of the husks I thought I detected a slight bruise—very small, but still it was there. It was just as if it had been caused by the insertion of some sharp instrument, and very, very carefully I began to probe. I thought I could follow it right down through the fibre—which was cut slightly— to the shell, and, with this to go on, I tried the same thing with other nuts. I was looking for something definite then, and I found it—sometimes more distinct than others. And I only found it in diseased nuts. It did not show at all in sound nuts.

"So what is the conclusion I have come to? I will tell you. In my opinion, this so-called disease which has attacked the coco-nuts on this coast is not the result of anything natural, but has been deliberately introduced by artificial means."

"Good heavens! How can that be?" asked Bailey.

"Ah! I don't know—yet. I'm only giving you my opinion. But look at this. I know from my own analysis that such a condition of hardening in the shell could be brought about by the artificial introduction of a chemical mixture. I don't know the exact composition of that mixture, but I am sure I could produce it in the laboratory. Very well—someone else may have hit on that same idea, and the result is an apparently mysterious disease which has attacked a large number of trees in this district, and, in the opinion of the residents here, threatens to wipe out the copra industry unless it can be checked. If I am right, it is no course of tree surgery that is required. On the contrary. It is human agency we must discover; and I shall go far enough even now to say that when we have found that agency the trouble will cease as suddenly as it began."

"Do you mean that some person, or persons, have introduced this so-called disease in order to create these coco-nut pearls?"

"Exactly. You have put the thing in a nutshell, if I may use the phrase without being accused of punning."

"But—but whom could it be?"

"Ah! That is our next step."

"Have you any suspicions?"

"Not definitely; but I have an idea of something. It has only been in my mind since Tinker returned from shooting muggers this evening. But it fits in to some extent with other information in my possession. I will explain. One of my enquiries was to find out what was becoming of all the rotten nuts. Each European on the station said he presumed they were just being thrown away. But a native dealer told me that the natives on whose topes they had been discovered were selling them at a trifling price to one of the big native millers—none other than Bamjee Haridee, who, it appears, is turning the rotten nuts and husks into fertiliser at his mill down the backwater. As far as I can discover, he is the only purchaser.

"But let us just imagine what this same Bamjee Haridee would say to himself if he came upon one of those pearls. Or, alternatively, let us try and suppose that this same astute gentleman might have known before he began to buy the rotten nuts what he had a chance of finding in a certain percentage of them. Wouldn't he be keen to keep the market to himself? Wouldn't he know that if the rotten nuts were bought by other dealers or crushers, they might light on the same thing? Therefore, wouldn't it be very much to his advantage to buy up all that were offered—to corner the market, as it were?"

"I'll say it would," agreed the engineer.

Blake looked at Tinker.

"Just where is that schooner lying at anchor, my lad?"

Tinker, who had been following Blake closely, grinned.

"Bang opposite Bamjee Haridee's mill jetty, guv'nor."

"I should have been willing to wager as much," said Blake.

Bailey looked puzzled at this remark, but Blake did not amplify it. Instead, he went on:

"Now, to get back to Green. Let us say that my tentative hypothesis is right—as far as it goes. Let us assume for the time being that there is a human agency behind this so-called disease which has attacked the nuts. All right. Supposing that person—who, we can take it, would be possessed of daring as well as brains— got to know that a mycologist was here investigating the trouble. Wouldn't he be greatly exercised, and wouldn't he try his best to stop him if he saw his scheme might be discovered and revealed before he had time to cash in as heavily as he wished?"

"Why, yes, I suppose so."

"Well, Bailey, that is exactly my idea. And that is why I do not think Green is lost—or, at least, did not lose himself. I believe that we have to look in another direction, rather than among the coco-nut topes, for Green. And I will go still further, and say that, in my opinion, when we have discovered just what human agency is behind this ingenious and destructive plot, we shall be on Green's track."

CHAPTER 8.   The Mycologist Pursues Investigations—Attacked By Natives—Bamjee Haridee's Prisoner.

HENRY GREEN, the mycologist who had official charge of the investigation of the strange disease which had attacked the coco-nut topes in Malabar, was an earnest young man with a very fine theoretical knowledge of his profession.

He had passed numerous very difficult examinations at college, had spent two years in research work at London University, and had shown great promise in his first appointment in the Tropical Agriculture Research Department in the Straits.

But his practical experience was still limited, and, up to the time when he had come to Malabar, he had never heard of the freak pearl which sometimes appeared in the coco-nut.

Therefore, it is not surprising that he tackled the problem along the lines which were best known to him, which were to begin with the roots of the tree, and make a variety of analyses from that starting point. A procedure with which Sexton Blake, under ordinary conditions, would have been in full agreement.

And eventually he must, too, have lit on just what Blake had found, but up to that time he had not done more than make a superficial examination of the diseased nuts which had come his way, and he had either not had the luck to find a pearl, or had not subjected the rotten mess inside the nuts to a sufficiently detailed examination.

However, he was making progress, and he had just reached the point where the clusters, the flower and the nuts would have been his next step, when he started across the backwater on the day when he seemed to have disappeared.

His movements up to the time when he left the motor-boat on the mainland side of the backwater are known; but from the time he entered the tope, there nothing was known of him.

Nor is it any wonder, for the young mycologist had not been working about among the trees without his movements being closely watched by certain very interested persons whose identity it is not difficult for the readers of this narrative to guess.

It was Bamjee Haridee who brought the news first to Huxton Rymer, and Rymer saw at once the danger to his plans. Things had just got nicely under way for him and Bamjee when the dealer brought the news, and then sat him down to hear what his European confederate had to say. Matters between Bamjee and Rymer had travelled a long way since that first day when Rymer had visited the native's mill.

Bamjee had not been slow to realise the glittering prospects which that glistening pearl offered—if Rymer could do what he said he could.

And Rymer had given proof that he was on certain ground. In the workroom on the schooner he had gathered about him certain chemicals, and for several days he had given himself up entirely to experiments.

Then had come the great moment when he had made his first test, and for a matter of three weeks or so he had been on tenterhooks to know the result.

It had been more than encouraging, and, forthwith, he and the native had gone into the thing to make a clean-up as quickly as possible. There was no question of one double-crossing the other.

Rymer had the secret and kept it; Bamjee had control of the necessary native labour. And so it was a fair fifty-fifty agreement.

No one among the native bazaar dealers, or the Europeans, seemed to think it odd that Bamjee Haridee was willing to buy the rotten nuts which the natives brought along to him in their little munjis. Everyone knew that Bamjee was a most progressive man, and that he was always getting into fresh things.

Therefore, when he allowed it to be known that he could turn out a low grade of fertilizer from the rotten nuts and husks, and thus could pay the native growers a small sum for them, he was looked upon as a real friend to the poor small grower in such a time of stress.

And not for one fleeting moment did Bamjee undeceive them. No, indeed, not he.

And so the merry game had gone on for a good three months before Henry Green and then Sexton Blake had arrived on the scene. So we come to the day when the young mycologist took himself and his tin boxes and instruments and notebooks across the backwater to pursue his investigations there.

He landed at a spot not very far from the mouth of the little creek where Tinker and Jack McGregor went the following day to shoot muggers. But he did not go in the direction of that creek. Instead, as soon as he was a short distance in from the edge of the water, he turned to the right and made an erratic way among the trees, his eyes raised towards the crowns of the trees on the look-out for nuts which would show signs of disease.

He stopped from time to time in order to examine a trunk, or to pick up and regard a nut which was lying on the ground. And when he came to a small group of coolies who were cutting nuts he stopped and picked out a couple of young ones which were obviously diseased. He slung these in his bag for later examination, and proceeded on his way.

Two minutes after he left the group of coolies, he might have been interested had he known that one of them sped swiftly to the edge of the backwater, and, standing there so that he could be seen from the other side, but not so that he was visible to the coolies in the boat which had brought the mycologist across, waved his arms as if signalling.

But a close observer might have seen a boat leave the jetty of Bamjee Haridee's mill a few minutes later, and start across the backwater, choosing a course that would bring it below Vendurthy Island.

But Green knew nothing of this, and kept on his way until he came to a small grove of young trees which he seemed to find of particular interest. He threw off his pack here and sat down in the shade to begin his examination of the nuts he had picked up on the way.

He was an efficient worker, and a swift handler of the knife, and in a space of time that would have done credit to a coolie, he had the husk sliced off, the nut opened up, and the greenish sticky-looking mass inside exposed to view.

This was the first occasion on which he had given his close attention to the mess inside the nut, and, in order to lose no portion of it, he opened up his shoulder case of tins, and proceeded to dig out the mass and place it in one of them.

It was while he was thus engaged when his fingers encountered something hard right up at one end of the nut, and in the very putrefying mess.

He hadn't the foggiest notion what it could be, but he was interested, and when he had detached it he performed the distasteful task of wiping off the evil-smelling slime in order to see just what it was.

And when he had it clean, the bespectacled eyes of the young mycologist goggled in sheer stupefaction. He had never heard of the freak condition of a coco-nut which can produce a pearl, but he thought he knew a pearl when he saw one; and he was quite certain that what he held between his finger and thumb at that moment was nothing else than such a gem. But how did it come there? he was asking himself.

He picked up the nut and examined it; he gave the same attention to the pieces of the husk. His thought just then was that he had lighted on the hidden loot of some criminal; that the pearl had been introduced into the nut which had been selected as a hiding-place.

But then his reason and common-sense told him this was impossible. He was quite certain the husk and shell had been perfectly normal when he opened them; that neither had been broken before. Then how in the name of all the "ics" and "isms" did that gem come inside the nut!

It might not be a true pearl, he told himself. On the other hand, his eyes and his reason told him it was. And then, being an intelligent young man, he thought why wasn't it possible for Nature to create a pearl in a diseased coco-nut in the same way in which it created one in the pearl oyster.

With an illuminating flash the truth burst upon him. He discovered in that moment the secret which others had discovered before him. And about three seconds later something else hit him with a physical force fully equal to the mental enlightment he had just received.

Henry Green had been so engrossed in his contemplation of the pearl that he had been entirely unaware that a small group of natives had been creeping upon him like shadows for the better part of ten minutes. There was a dozen or so in the mob and they dodged from tree to tree with the rapidity and silence which the Red Indian of America was won't to employ with such mastery.

One by one, they collected behind the tree beneath which the mycologist sat, and it was just at the moment when he made his great discovery that one of the group gave a signal. With one accord the mob dashed in upon him coming from behind and overwhelming him before he had the faintest suspicion what was afoot.

But Green's time at college had not been entirely spent in the laboratories, and the class-rooms. He had taken a healthily active interest in athletics, and, while he had not shone particularly in any one sport, he had been a good sound team man in many. He had done quite a little boxing, too, and when he felt the physical weight crushing down upon him he was quite intelligent enough to realise that, for some reason unknown to him he was being attacked.

He came into action while he was still being flattened. In some way, he managed to throw off those who were on his back, and, staggering to his knees, he got his fists working.

He drove in blow after blow until he broke the mob before him, and then he managed to get to his feet. He retreated instinctively until he felt the trunk of the tree against his back, and then he fought a hard defensive battle.

He had no idea what the object of the assault was. But he knew there must be some very definite purpose behind the mob instrument to make them attack a European in such open fashion in broad daylight, even if it was in a secluded tope where no other European was likely to pass.

But he was wise enough not to pause then to ask for an explanation. He had sent two of the coolies down, and, as the lust of battle rose in him, he advanced a little and took the offensive.

This determined resistance on the part of one whom they had thought entirely at their mercy rather flabbergasted the natives for a bit, and they retreated before the rain of blows which came upon them with such punishing rapidity.

Green fixed on one who was bigger than the others, and who seemed to carry about him an air of surly authority. He drove a way through to this fellow and hammered him viciously on the body, then feinted with his right and wound up with a perfect left to the point of the chin.

The fellow went down as if a club had hit him, and at this some confusion seemed to arise among the others. They gave way before the fresh onslaught which Green carried among them, and it looked for a few moments as if they would turn tail and fly. But at that critical moment a sharp whistle sounded off among the trees, and, as if it were a command, they gathered together and came on in a fresh bunched rush.

Their sheer weight drove Green back against the tree, and, while he handed out severe punishment, he knew he could not bear up for long if they kept at it.

Once again the whistle sounded, and for the second time it acted as a spur. They closed in on him and suddenly one of them hurled a coco-nut full at him. It struck him with terrific force between the eyes, and he went down.

He struggled with all his will-power to keep control of his reeling senses, but the brain had been tapped too hard, and, still clawing feebly at the air, he fell forward, unconscious.

With the white man lying helpless the mob was courageous enough. With grunts which might have meant anything, they threw themselves upon him, and in a trice had him securely bound with bits of coir rope. Then they picked him up and carried him off through the trees.

As they went ahead another native suddenly appeared. Evidently it was he who had whistled on his pack when they had faltered, for he made an authoritative gesture and motioned for the coolies to carry their burden after him. He was a big native, obviously one in some authority. He wore a clean white *dhootie*, and the shirt, coat, and waistcoat of an European— the shirt, after the native fashion, hanging outside the dhootie.

He also wore a gold-edged turban on his head and carried an umbrella—hall-mark of the native of substance. He was, in fact, one of Bamjee Haridee's foremen, and to him had been entrusted the little expedition which the native dealer had organised against the mycologist.

He led the way eastward until he came to the bank of one of the numerous small creeks which empty into the backwater. It was the next one to that which Tinker and Jack McGregor were to go up the following day. Against the bank here was a good-sized wallum, which was the same that had put out from the mill jetty when the coolie had signalled across the backwater.

Into this the prone form of the mycologist was dumped, and then half a dozen empty copra sacks were drawn over him to conceal him from view. With a word to his men to stand by, the foreman went back to where the attack had taken place, and kicked the native there into consciousness.

As the fellow stumbled to his feet, the foreman urged him with his foot in the direction of the creek, and then he himself set about to collect all the mycologist's paraphernalia. He was thus engaged when he came upon the pearl which Green had been examining when the attack came, and which had fallen into the grass.

The foreman's eyes glistening as he regarded it, and since he had received no instruction which covered that, he lifted his dhootie and, smiling slyly, concealed the gem in the loin cloth which he wore beneath.

Then he gave a last look round to see that nothing had been left, and with his load returned to where his men were waiting. He dumped his burden into one end of the wallum and motioned for one of the coolies to throw an empty sack over it. Then he raised his umbrella and took his seat.

The crew piled in after him, and the last man in pushed off. Four of them took paddles and backed the wallum down the creek until they reached the backwater. There they swung it round and drove it ahead towards the lower end of Vendurthy.

Passing the island, they headed for a small creek on the lower side of the mill. On the right bank of this little creek, which was more of an artificial canal than it was creek, was the main wall of the mill godown in which three doors had been built.

From these doors copra or oil could be loaded into wallums, as well as from the jetty in front. Then on the left bank was the wall of Bamjee Haridee's house—a big, rambling structure built of thick walls of laterite.

In this wall was one door which gave on to the creek, and it was before this the wallum drew up. The foreman got out and lowered his umbrella. Then he tapped on the door and waited. Soon there was the sound of shuffling footsteps inside, and a second later the door opened. Inside was a native servant, and just behind him Bamjee Haridee himself.

A look passed between him and the foreman, and, as if in answer to a question, the latter nodded as he salaamed. The dealer spoke a few curt words, and several of the crew of the wallum, after a swift look in the direction of the backwater, lifted out the unconscious form of the mycologist, empty copra sacks and all.

With a rapid movement they passed him through the doorway, and then two more threw in his paraphernalia.

The door slammed, and Bamjee led the way along a flower-bordered walk, through a big gateway into a beautiful garden beyond, where a fountain was playing in the midst of all the riot of colour. Large trees gave grateful shade, and over on the right was the long trellis-work veranda which showed where the woman's quarters were situated.

The unconscious mycologist was carried in behind this trellis-work, and up some stairs to the floor above. Here he was placed in a small room at the very back of the purdah quarters, and, as he closed the door upon him, Bamjee Haridee gave a grunt as if pleased with a job well done.

As indeed he might well have been, for the quarters of the native purdah women are absolutely taboo in India, and under no circumstances would their privacy be violated.

It was just that law which the British Raj respect and insists on all others respecting that Bamjee had bent to his purpose, and the young mycologist might just as well have been dropped into the bottom of the sea for all the hint the outer world would get of what had happened to him.

Unless something very unusual should occur.

CHAPTER 9.   What Passed Between Bamjee and Rymer—Mary Trent's Warning.

IT was well after dark on the night following the day on which the mycologist had been abducted that Bamjee Haridee stowed his fat carcass in the stern-sheets of his small motor-boat and ordered his serang to drive the craft across to where the schooner La Sylvide lay at anchor.

As he mounted the short ladder and went over the side he saw a blur of white on the poop deck, which he guessed correctly was the European, Rymer and the memsahib. He waddled aft and Rymer rose to meet him. Mary Trent did not rise, and when the dealer salaamed she bowed coldly enough, for Mary did not like Mr. Bamjee Haridee, and would be far better pleased when Rymer's business with the man was finished.

However, Rymer was not so squeamish in his choice of confederates so long as there was money at the end of the game, so with a word of apology to Mary he led his visitor down the companionway to the saloon below. Both the cook and the chokra had been given bazaar leave for the evening, so there was no one about but Mary, and it didn't matter what she might overhear.

Bamjee had come to make the evening settlement of the gems which had been found during the day. In the opening of the nuts and the division of the pearls, Rymer was forced to take the dealer more or less on trust; for, were he to be seen hanging about the mill too much it would be bound to leak through the bazaar, and thence into the offices of the Europeans— the last thing either of them wanted while they were playing such a ticklish game.

But Rymer knew pretty well how many nuts were opened during the day, and he had figured to a nicety about what percentage of "finds" there should be, so he could check up Bamjee more or less accurately. And if the dealer tried to hold back any on him, why— well, Rymer issued the "dope" for the nuts each evening after the division, and he could stop that at any time.

The secret was his and his only, and without it Bamjee would get nary a pearl. So it paid him from a purely financial point of view to play straight.

On this occasion the day's result was somewhat less than usual, consisting of but thirty-seven pearls in all, and, with the exception of

58

five, they were more or less of a disappointing size. Good enough for ordinary commercial requirements, but not enough to fetch the big prices which were in Rymer's mind.

However, he checked up the list which Bamjee submitted, and then the division took place. With their usual practice, when necessary, they tossed a coin for the odd large pearl, which, as usual, Rymer won. In that little part of the business there was never the slightest doubt in his mind who would be the winner. And Bamjee seemed to accept it philosophically enough.

Then the dealer mentioned a certain matter which was occupying their minds to a considerable extent. This was the responsibility of the mycologist, who still lay a prisoner in the purdah part of Bamjee's house.

Bamjee had been from the first all for bundling him into one of the pattimars which would be sailing soon, and have him dumped on to the Laccadives where—it was a safe bet—he would languish for at least six months before he found a chance to come back to the coast. By that time, he argued, their little business would be completed, and Rymer would be gone.

Bamjee had not the slightest fear that Green would ever find out who had instigated the attack on him, or where he had been kept, prisoner. He had not seen where he had been brought, for the simple reason that he had been unconscious. And before he had fully regained consciousness he had been given a native drug which would be fed to him at intervals for all the time he was held a prisoner. Which was the acme of simplicity from Bamjee's point of view.

But Rymer opposed this. He knew only too well that a dozen different things might happen, and if Green should get back to the coast before they had finished their business, things might become more than awkward. So he was strongly in favour of having the mycologist kept just where he was for some time longer.

Bamjee had found it possible to stretch his caste conscience sufficiently under this urge of necessity to put the prisoner where he knew no Europeans or other officials would ever penetrate; but, at the same time, the fact remained that all the time he was within the *zenana* the place was being polluted, and during that time Bamjee could not, according to the tenets of his religion, enjoy the society of any of his wives, a thing which annoyed him, for at heart the old rascal was strongly domestic. Besides, his latest wife was more delectable than the finest pearl they had found so far, and it pained him that he must forego her fascinating society.

For the second evening they had failed to agree on this subject when Rymer changed it.

"We will both think it over to-night, and come to a decision to-morrow," he said. "There is something else of which I wish to speak to you. It may mean further complications. This is what it is:

"This evening, just before dusk, the memsahib and I were leaning over the stern rail when a small munji came along. In it were two European lads. They had been shooting somewhere down the backwater. One of them I had never seen before, but the other I recognised as a young fellow I knew quite well. It means, if he is staying in Cochin, that there is a man, my most deadly enemy, staying there as well—or near there. Have you ever heard of a man known as Sexton Blake? He is an English detective who has been in India many times."

"Sexton Blake—yes, I have heard of him," answered Bamjee. "He comes to the coast sometimes with Congrove Sahib of the Madras police."

"That is the man," rejoined Rymer. "Well, if he is in Cochin, what is he doing here? Is he here on pleasure? Or is it business? We know there has been a good deal of inquiry going on over what they think is the strange disease which has attacked the coco-nut trees here. We know that is why the other man was here. We have disposed of him for the time being; but if this man Sexton Blake is on the same game—well, it will be a very different proposition. At any rate, I shall not rest easy until I know just what he is doing here. If he is on the same business, then we shall have to stop him—quick! Do you understand, Bamjee? The work must be done without any delay—before he has a chance to smell out the truth."

"You think he could be dangerous?"

"I don't think it—I know it. You can take it from me that I do not talk like that without having good reason."

"No, I believe you, my friend," rejoined Bamjee. "You are not the sort of sahib who frightens easily. But it will be easy enough for me to find out what this man is doing in Cochin. The bazaar will know everything, and I can find out this very night."

"And act?"

"At once. What would you have me do?"

"Anything that is necessary that will drive him out of the place, or cause him to drop this business, if that is what has brought him here."

"It shall be done. Do you think it would be wise to do with him as we have done with the young fool who fell into our hands so easily?"

"No—no—no! He is an entirely different proposition. He must be driven from the place—or—" And Rymer stopped significantly.

"He shall be driven out," said Bamjee confidently. "I have many ways—there are many people who obey me. I can have done what I wish, and this man shall soon go. Do not fear. It shall be done!"

Rymer nodded and was content, for he knew the dealer did control an enormous underground power in the place.

Therefore, he knew that if Bamjee promised that Sexton Blake should be dealt with, he would do it by some subtle Eastern means.

Shortly after that the dealer took his departure. When he was gone, and the cessation of the staccato "chucka-a-chuck" of the engine announced that he had reached his own jetty, Rymer told Mary what had passed. Mary listened in silence, then she said:

"I have no doubt that he can use some means against Sexton Blake, but I should feel more confident of the result if it were a straight out-and-out fight between you and Sexton Blake. I tell you, I do not like Bamjee Haridee. How many pearls have we for our share now?"

"Something over three hundred, my dear."

"Isn't that enough for now? They must be worth quite a lot."

"They are; but I have set my heart on a clean five hundred, and I'll stick it until then. Don't you worry, my dear girl. I can't see why you should feel nervous about Bamjee. I can play just as deep a game as that old bird."

"Yes, but a different type,"

"But what can he do?"

"He might double-cross us."

"Double-cross us! With whom, for goodness' sake?"

"Well, with Sexton Blake for one."

Rymer laughed softly.

"What strange fancies you have, Mary. Blake is the last person Bamjee would hook up with; and, besides, I hold him hard. He can't do a thing without the dope I give him, and, to be sure, there is no one who knows the secret of that but myself and—you."

He took her hand and pressed it gently, and for some time they sat in silence, the girl's eyes gazing up past the bazaar front where the lights were reflected on the black face of the water. Rymer was smoking, and must have been dreaming, for he gave a start when Mary spoke again.

"I may be wrong; but don't forget, my dear man, there is something in a woman's intuition. You watch that fat dealer. I won't speak of it again, but I have a feeling that he will double-cross you if he gets the chance. And then I should have to take a hand, for if he harmed you I should place three little pellets of lead in the thickest part of his body." Then she laughed a little shakily as she slipped her hand from his and rose. "But perhaps I am suffering from a touch of fever," she added. "I am going down now, and take five grains of quinine. Perhaps I shall feel differently about things in the morning."

She disappeared then, leaving Rymer to mull over what she had said. Again he laughed softly at the thought of Bamjee double-crossing him. But he would have done well to heed what Mary had said, for, curiously enough, the first germ of that idea was just entering the cunning mind of the dealer.

And some strange events were to occur before morning came.

CHAPTER 10.   The Native Cunning of Bamjee—Strange Happenings in the Night.

BAMJEE HARIDEE was a quick worker. And, unlike a good many natives, he knew his own mind.

On leaving the schooner he landed at his own mill jetty, and made his way through the compound, outside which he found his private rickshaw waiting. He stepped in and grunted an order, and the under-sized rickshaw coolie went speeding along towards the bazaar in a way that seemed incredible in one of his frail build.

The rickshaw drew up in front of Bamjee's extensive bazaar premises, and the dealer entered. In the outer office several clerks were at work, for it was now getting late in the evening, and the real life of the bazaar was just beginning.

Bamjee devoted himself for some time to an examination of the various transactions that had taken place during his absence, and from time to time went into conference with other dealers who came to see him. It was rarely indeed that Bamjee went to them. He would condescend to visit Europeans in their offices, but in his own realm he was almost supreme.

On that particular night things were comparatively quiet, so, after issuing instructions regarding purchases and sales in the copra and coco-nut oil market, Bamjee entered his private office.

When he had squatted down before his little box-like desk he clapped his hands, and a young native entered. The man was a close relative of Bamjee's on his wife's side, and hence to be trusted, for Bamjee's good was his good, as he well knew. Bamjee talked with him in low tones for some minutes, and then the young native went out.

He took up his little round embroidered cap, and, leaving the office, stepped into a rickshaw. He drove straight through the bazaar until he came to the European quarter, and kept on there until he was past the maidan and right in the middle of the Fort, where most of the European bungalows were situated.

He left the rickshaw at a dark corner and proceeded on foot. His course took him along until he was in a small open space just opposite the bungalow which was being occupied by Bailey, the engineer with whom Sexton Blake and Tinker were staying.

The bungalow was a very old one, built away back at the time of the Dutch occupation of Cochin, and hence the walls were of very thick laterite, with the living quarters upstairs. The ground-floor was composed simply of godowns which one reached by way of a passage that ran right through the centre of the house to the compound at the back.

There were the servants' quarters and the kitchens. The godowns on the ground-floor were seldom used in these days except by the servants.

The veranda was lighted, and, as he lurked in the shadow, the native could hear the murmur of voices. Between the road and the house there was a narrow stretch of garden, not more than twenty feet in depth, the entrance being between two high swing gates which would admit a rickshaw or a "push-push" (quaint type of four-wheeled vehicle which is to be seen only in Southern India).

The boundary wall was low and thick. The great risk would be dogs, which, the watcher knew, were usually to be found in considerable force at every European bungalow, and which invariably had a rooted aversion to every native who was not actually known to them. But that was a risk he would have to take.

He waited until the voices rose a little higher on the veranda; then he was over the wall like a shadow, and went creeping across the garden until he came to the dark mouth of the passage which led through to the compound. He slid into that, and, as he passed the foot of the stairs which led to the veranda above, he heard the sudden growl of a dog upstairs.

But he did not wait for the animal to find him. He went through the passage swiftly and noiselessly, and then, as he reached the compound, he saw a single light burning in the kitchen quarters and heard the low murmur of voices. Some of the servants, at least, were still up.

He crossed the compound, and suddenly thrust his head in at the door of the kitchen. The cook, the butler, and the chokra were there, squatting on the ground, chewing betel and gossiping, and all three shrank back as the head appeared in the doorway.

But the visitor made a sound for silence and motioned to the butler to get up. The man did so, and, at a low word from the other, led the way along and into one of the godowns, which was as black as the lowest Hindu pit.

Then the young native began to speak, and the boy listened

respectfully, for anyone connected with the powerful Bamjee Haridee was one to be feared. When the other had finished the boy spoke a few words, and then, for some five minutes or so, their conversation consisted of questions and answers. At the end of that time the visitor touched the boy on the shoulder and hissed:

"It is understood, then—send the chokra out at once, and see that the word is passed to the servants at every other bungalow, and at the club. You will attend to matters here. Be on the watch for me, for I shall probably return. It is for my master to decide what shall be done."

The boy answered that he would obey, and the young man prepared to take his leave. He went through the passage as noiselessly as he had come, and, speeding across the garden, slid over the wall and faded away among the shadows. But the big Airedale terrier upstairs had been again made suspicious by his passing, and this time he began barking in some excitement.

Bailey was not on the veranda at the time, but Sexton Blake and Tinker were there, and, knowing that something must have aroused the animal, Blake walked to the head of the stairs and looked down.

Then he called to the boy. At once the butler's voice came up from the darkness.

"Yes, sahib?"

"The dog has been disturbed by something," said Blake sharply. "What are you doing down there?"

"Nothing, master," lied the boy smoothly. "I was just seeing that the store cupboard was safely locked. There are bandicoots about, master."

And while Blake was not at all inclined to believe him, he knew that there would be no use in looking for the cause of the dog's suspicions now. So, with a shrug, he went back to his seat.

In the meantime, the young native had sped round the corner, and was once more in the rickshaw on his way to the bazaar. As soon as he reached his destination, he went at once to Bamjee's private office, where the latter was waiting for him. He made his report, and when he had finished the dealer nodded approvingly.

"You have done well," he commended him. "Now, let me think."

Bamjee stuffed a big wad of betel nut and leaf and lime in his mouth, and, while he rolled it round and round in his cheek, he set himself to tackle the problem of how to deal with the matter, which must be handled quickly.

He had already laid the fuse, so to say, but it needed something more than that— something which would convince the Europeans on the station as well. The native servants were simple enough to handle.

He pondered on the thing for the better part of half an hour, and then suddenly he turned to where his young relative stood meekly waiting. He shot a question at him, then another and another, and, finally, he wagged his head in the native way of meaning "that will do." He issued certain definite instructions to which the young man listened carefully; then Bamjee waved his hand, and the other departed once more.

Again he entered the rickshaw, and this time he drove through to the house of a certain bazaar dealer who traded in all sorts of odd junk. He made a purchase there of an extraordinary nature, and, even though the price was only a couple of rupees, the haggling consumed nearly an hour before a figure was agreed upon.

Then, with his purchase in a small basket, he re-entered the rickshaw, and for the second time went speeding along towards the European quarter.

Bamjee was springing his little plot to "fix" Sexton Blake.

TINKER'S bed-room was a back room on the right-hand side of
the bungalow, which was small, and had, at some time in the past,
been built on as a sort of annex. It was just over the compound and
opposite the kitchen quarters, and, as the roof was only of palm-leaf
thatching, he could, when he was in the room, hear practically
everything that went on down below.

Just back of this was the smaller room where his galvanised bath-
tub was placed, and from this a narrow flight of wooden steps led
down into the compound, for the use of the water-man and the
sweeper-woman when attending to him.

From the front of his room he passed straight into what was now
the dining-room, but which had originally been a dark, windowless
store-room, used probably as such by the original Dutch occupants of
the bungalow.

Just outside the windows of Tinker's room there was a large gold
mohor-tree, which was a great rendezvous for crows during the day,
and from which Tinker used to pick off one or two daily with a small
.22 rifle. At the foot of this tree was a square well, from which the
water for the baths was drawn.

The drinking water and that used for cooking was brought daily
in a great cask from Ernakulam, on the other side of the backwater, to
which place it was piped fourteen miles from the Alwaye River. So
difficult is it to get safe drinking water in Cochin; and, even at that,
every drop had to be boiled.

This brief description is necessary in order to follow clearly the
events which took place that night.

It was nearly midnight when Blake, Tinker, and Bailey retired.
Blake had said little more on the subject of the pearls after giving his
opinion as to the direction in which they would eventually find they
would have to look for the missing mycologist. But there had been the
plans for the morrow to discuss and arrangements to make.

Blake's bed-room was on the same side of the bungalow where
Bailey's quarters were situated, so when Tinker bade them goodnight
he went off to the other side alone. There were two dogs in the
place—one the Airedale which had shown signs of uneasiness twice
during the evening, and a pretty, ancient old "pi" spaniel that was

both lazy and deaf.

The Airedale trotted off after Bailey and Blake, and the spaniel waddled along after Tinker, who looked at it in humorous disapproval as he picked up a couple of pieces of sugar on his way through the dining-room.

"This is what comes of feeding you when I shouldn't," he remarked, as he sat on the edge of his bed and handed the animal a bit of the sweet stuff. "You see, if I hadn't succumbed to-day and given you that stuff at tiffin, you wouldn't have followed me in here to-night. You would have gone off with your pal the Airedale. You are a pretty shrewd old fellow at that, but it's no wonder you are so fat if you eat all the time and never take any exercise. I'll bet a rupee a bandicoot could run right over your tail and you wouldn't even woof at him."

The deaf old spaniel hadn't the foggiest notion what Tinker was talking about, but he could see that he was speaking, and probably the rumble of his voice reached him. At any rate, the dog wagged his bit of a tail and shoved up his muzzle for more sugar, which he promptly received.

But the rumble of Tinker's voice reached farther than the confines of the little room. It was heard in the compound below, and while he was sitting there talking to the dog the butler stole out of the shadow of one of the godowns and stood listening.

He was still standing there when Tinker blew out his light and slipped under the mosquito netting.

It took only about five minutes for Tinker to drop off to sleep, for he had had a long day, and was comfortably tired. The spaniel was streached out on the floor close to the bed snoring before the lad was, and just then the butler crept softly up the steps at the back to listen. Satisfied, he retreated, and performed the same spying duty on the other side.

He could not get near Blake's bed-room, for it was half-way along towards the front, but he could listen at the door shutters of Bailey's room, and there was no doubt that the engineer was well asleep, for he was snoring mightily. The Airedale, as it happened, had taken up its place in Blake's room.

Then for nearly an hour silence reigned over the bungalow. It was getting on for one o'clock when a silent shadow came over the front wall, and glided along across the garden to the passage leading to the compound. It vanished there, but a few seconds later there was a whispering at the entrance of one of the godowns, and then first one and another, and another shadow came out and slipped through the passage towards the front gates.

There was the chokra and the kitchen "matey," next went the cook and the house "matey", after them the waterman and the mali; and finally, the sweeper woman, and a rickshaw man, who had been sleeping at the bungalow. The punkah men did not sleep at the bungalow, and had already departed.

That left only the butler, and the person who had just come over the wall, and the pair stood in the shadow while the other servants, with their belongings in little bundles, crept out and disappeared into the night.

It was a general exodus, and the three Europeans upstairs were entirely ignorant of the proceedings going on below while they slept.

Once, as it happened, the Airedale lifted his head and sniffed suspiciously, but he must have recognised the scent of the servants known to him, for after an uneasy movement he lay down again, apparently satisfied.

Then the butler and the new arrival whispered together again, and finally the butler also stole after his fellow servants. That left the stranger alone, and when the "boy" had quite disappeared, he crept along until he was in the compound.

He stole across and stood under the wide-spreading mohor tree, which grew by the well. He remained there like a statue for the space of full ten minutes or so; then he began to proceed on his purpose, silently as only a native can move.

Something was hanging on his arm, which seemed to give him a little trouble, for he shifted it back from time to time. But, despite this, he made not a sound as he began to climb into the tree. Up he went, feeling his way with infinite precaution until he was in the branches just on a level with the eaves of the bungalow, and a little higher than the windows of Tinker's bedroom, which were just opposite him.

In fact, so close was he that he could hear the lad snoring inside, for the windows were wide open.

He remained there for some little time, for he knew that, even though no one had been roused so far, there was a subtle "something" that creeps through the night to sleeping persons which, without any apparent reason, may rouse them. He knew the value of letting the vibrations of the night get his "feel," so to say.

It was nearly a quarter of an hour later before he continued his progress. Now, he turned to the right, and began creeping along a thick branch towards the front roof of the house which Tinker's annex room joined. He felt cautiously there to see if there were any loose tiles, but seemed satisfied, for after a little he crept cautiously across.

He gripped his naked toes into the edge of the gutter, and with his hand pressed flat, well ahead of him, and at first, touching very lightly, he began to go up the sloping roof as stealthily as a panther.

Once he touched a loose tile, and at this he flattened himself close to the slope. He heard nothing, but still he lay there, scarcely breathing, until he thought it safe to proceed. Then on again, and so up and up, until his groping fingers went over the top ridge of the roof. He pulled himself up until he was astride, and then he swung his little basket round in front of him.

He opened the lid, and thrusting in his hand, took out something. It seemed to flutter, as it were, in his hand, but he held it firmly, and then busied himself rubbing his hand back and forth at one spot. When he had finished, he brought his free hand round and placed the thing he carried on the spot where he had been rubbing. He held it there for a few minutes, and then, ever so slowly, he loosened his hold.

There was the sound of fluttering again, but as he took his hand away, the thing he had placed there remained, and he prepared to descend.

The basket had now served its purpose, but still he stuck to it. He could have heaved it away as far as the adjoining compound, but he did not do so. He slung it behind him, and began his descent, going as slowly and with as great care as he had come up.

It was just at that moment that Tinker, who was dreaming that he was being pursued by a full score of angry muggers, not one of which was less than forty feet in length, felt something touching his arm.

In his nightmare he thought it was one of the pursuing muggers just nosing him before clamping its ten feet teeth into him, and so vivid was the impression, that he came out of his dream in a cold sweat of terror. It was a wonder he did not cry out.

He turned over and, still under the influence of the nightmare, felt his heart go into his mouth as his hand encountered something. That brought him wide awake, and then he discovered what it was that had been nosing him. It was the muzzle of the spaniel pressing through the mosquito noting, urgently, insistently.

Tinker patted the dog's nose, and whispered:

"Go to sleep, you greedy old thing. What the dickens do you mean waking me up at this hour of the night for more sugar. You'll bust, that's what will happen to you."

But the old dog was not satisfied. He still kept pushing at Tinker's arm with his muzzle, and then, suddenly, Tinker sat perfectly rigid as a sound came from, it seemed, just outside his window.

It was a sort of clatter, then a rattle, and finally a thud, and as he listened to it Tinker thought to himself:

"Now that sounded just exactly like a loose tile sliding off the roof and falling down into the compound. But it is a calm night to-night, and those heavy tiles do not go floating about unless some human agency or a pretty high wind disturbs them. I wonder if that is why the old dog is trying to wake me. I'll just have a look-see."

He gently lifted the mosquito-net and, laying a cautioning hand on the dog, slid out of bed. He crept across the room until he was close by the open windows. There were four of them altogether, and swung inward on hinges, which left practically the whole of that side of the chamber open to the night.

The branches of the mohor tree swept right across against the outside, and, standing as he was, Tinker was more or less screened, although he could peer through the openings between the branches.

It was a clear, starry night, but there was no moon. He could see fairly well, however, for in that part of the world the stars are very bright, and he knew he was not a victim of his imagination when he saw a blur about half-way up the roof of the main part of the bungalow.

Now, tiles do not suddenly grow bulgy in the night like sponges sucking up water, and Tinker knew it. Nor was that blur caused by any shadow from the mohor tree. It was something solid and definite and sinister. It was, he knew, a human being, or an animal, flattened on the tiles, motionless.

And he needed nothing more to tell him that there was the cause of the tile slipping down and falling into the compound. How the old dog had sensed it he couldn't guess, but something other than his hearing had told him that things were not as they should be.

A younger dog would have started barking; the old stager

attracted the attention of the white man he had adopted, for experience had taught him that all things were settled by those masters.

Tinker crouched and watched. Lying flat against the tiles, the native, who had struck a loose tile with his toe, and sent it clattering down into the compound, was as motionless as the dead. Inwardly, he was cursing in whatever variety of oaths he most favoured, at the accident, but as the minutes passed and no one seemed to have been roused, he thought it safe to start on his downward journey once more.

Just then there came the double hoot of an owl, and so close was the cry, that Tinker almost betrayed his close presence in jumping. The sound, too, seemed to make the roof prowler hesitate, but then, as things again grew silent, he began slipping ever so slowly downwards, so slowly that it might have been the shadow caused by the almost imperceptible sweep of a branch of the mohor tree.

Tinker watched him. He knew now it was no toddy cat which at first he thought it might have been, for those obscene creatures are great roof prowlers, and there were some, as he knew, living up round the eaves of the main part of the bungalow. But this was a human being, a prowling native, and, as such, Tinker prepared to deal with him.

At first he felt inclined to send out a hail that would waken the servants, but then he decided to capture the intruder himself, for, he reasoned, it might be one of their own servants up to some sort of mischief, though what he could find to do on the roof he couldn't guess.

He laid another cautioning hand on the spaniel's muzzle, and edged a little closer to the window. He had figured out how he would attack, but he wanted to wait until his man came into the tree, which he must do in order to reach the ground. He stood like a statue while the prowler came on down and reached the gutter at the edge. Then, at the very moment when he swung out into the tree, Tinker performed exactly the same action.

Lightly, he went over the sill and, catching hold of the nearest branch of the mohor tree, swung himself out. His groping bare toes found a foothold, and he had just steadied himself when the native, now fully aware that he was discovered, came crashing down upon him.

Tinker took the assault with his shoulder. He felt the other give a grunt of pain as he checked him full in the abdomen, then Tinker braced his legs against the trunk and branches of the tree, got his hands free and reached up.

The other seemed nothing loath to come to grips. As far as position went, he certainly had the advantage, for he was standing a foot or so higher than Tinker. Also, his feet were like bits of leather, and the sharp protuberances on the branches were as nothing to him, whereas they dug into Tinker's tender soles like blunt nails, causing him no end of discomfort.

But he stuck grimly to his task, and, as the native swept bang down into him, his arm shooting in for a stranglehold, Tinker brought his right fist up in a sweeping blow that caught the native once more in the abdomen. And no native is strong there.

He gave another grunt of pain, but had plenty of grit, for he plunged in again, and this time he got a hold round Tinker's shoulders.

Hanging on thus, and almost precipitating them both to the ground, he swung his feet clear and dropped lower until he could entwine his legs round Tinker's calves.

Tinker rocked back, and for a second, it seemed that they must both plunge down through the branches. But somehow they recovered, and as Tinker felt the strong sinewy fingers of his antagonist digging into his throat, he knew he would have to come across with an effective counter soon or he would be strangled like a chicken.

So engrossed was he in the struggle, and, so much racket were they making among the branches, that he did not know the little spaniel had gone dashing through the dining-room and on to the front veranda, barking furiously. Nor did he know that the Airedale had joined in, and that Blake and Bailey had both been roused by the racket the dogs were making.

He had no time for that. There was something about the silent fury of the native with whom he was struggling that told him it was no ordinary night prowler he had surprised.

He could not guess who the fellow was, but, as those black fingers dug deeper and deeper into his throat, a heavy rage seized Tinker and, reckless of whether they plunged to the ground or not, he began coming in with both fists.

He drove in a left, right, left, right to the body, and the fury of his tattoo forced the native to loosen his hold. Tinker jerked his head back, and brought his right fist up sharply in a short jab to the chin. He followed with the left, and then, as the native lurched forward in another desperate attempt to reach his throat, Tinker sent in a terrific smashing blow to the face.

It sent the Indian back hard against the trunk of the tree, but he rebounded and came down with all his weight. He was now as reckless as Tinker of consequences, for, unlike the lad, he had heard the sound of the dogs barking, and knew the others in the bungalow would be roused. He went into the lad like a jungle fury, and, despite his every effort, Tinker was forced back.

He made a grab at the branch to steady himself, and succeeded for the moment. Then he drove in a hard left again, but it grazed off the body, and again the native was in close. His full weight was behind his arms, and, as Tinker heaved himself back to avoid those clutching fingers, he felt his foot slip. He made a wild effort to save himself, recovered for a moment and managed to get his hands about the other's shoulders. Then his feet slipped off the branch.

He hung on like grim death, felt the other yield and come downwards with him. Then the native seemed to get a grip that held him, and, although he tried with every atom of strength to hang on, Tinker felt his arms coming down over the other's body, his waist, and then his thighs.

He clutched wildly at the native's calves. His fingers clung for a little about his ankles, and this time he swung clear with his full weight dragging down. He felt the native's feet come jerking off the branch, and he must have been hanging only by his hands, for they both lurched out free among the branches.

Then Tinker's hands gave, and he felt himself start plunging down through the branches. He seemed to have dragged the other loose in his last wild grab, but he could not make sure, and the next instant it did not matter.

Down he went like a falling coco-nut. Through the lower branches of the mohor tree he plunged, and then he struck the curbing of the well with terrific force. He rebounded from this, as his fingers clutched wildly at thin air; then he felt himself falling still again, and the next thing he knew was that he was into and under the slimy water of the well.

CHAPTER 12.   Further Happenings in the Night—A Fierce Tussle—Tragedy—Mystifying Circumstances.

SEXTON BLAKE came awake at the barking of the dogs. He heard them kicking up a row on the front veranda, and, knowing that something more than a fugitive bandicoot must have roused them, he lifted the mosquito curtain and slid out of bed.

He thrust his feet into his slippers, and, stumbling across the room, found the lantern which he had been using instead of a candle. The matches were on the table beside it, and, in a few seconds, he had it lit.

He clamped down the chimney and called to the dogs. They came running in under the half doors which shielded his room from the view of anyone on the veranda, but still permitted a free current of air to pass. They were vastly excited, and, as soon as they saw that they had his attention, they started back towards the veranda.

At that moment Bailey came stumbling in through the dressing-room that separated his room from Blake's.

"What is it?" he asked sleepily. "What are those dogs kicking up such a devil of a row about?"

"Hanged if I know," answered Blake. "But I am going to find out. Are you coming?"

"Sure. Let's see what it is."

With the lantern Blake led the way out on to the veranda, and was starting down the stairs, but the dogs showed that they wanted to go the other way. The spaniel was most insistent, and, knowing that they were the safest guides to follow, Blake swung in through the living-room and on towards the dining-room, the dogs running on ahead.

They passed through the dining-room, but, instead of making through the service-door to the back veranda, which looked into the compound, the spaniel led the way into Tinker's room. Wonderingly, Blake and Bailey followed, and then, as he entered the lad's room, Blake gave an exclamation of surprise, for he could see that the bed there was empty.

The spaniel had trotted across to the window, and was showing signs of excitement there. Blake crossed the room and, holding the lantern high, peered out. Then, suddenly he gave a start and cried:

Good heavens! Bailey, there is someone hanging by the neck between two branches of this tree."

He turned and hurried through the bedroom. Passing through that he jerked open the door leading to the back stairs. He kept calling for the servants as he went down, and Bailey's voice joined in. As they reached the bottom and were just turning round towards the tree, they both paused and stood listening as a sound reached them. Again it came, and like a flash Blake swung towards the well.

"That was Tinker," he said over his shoulder. "Come here, Bailey." Then he held the lantern out, and down as far as he could, and peered down into the well. "Hallo! Hallo!" he called. "What is it?"

"It's me, guv'nor," came Tinker's voice faintly. "I'm down here in the bottom of the well. Up to my neck and hanging on by my fingers. Can't hold on much longer."

Blake did not wait to ask how the lad had come into such an extraordinary position at that hour of the night, or, rather, the morning. Instead, he turned to Bailey and rapped:

"Dig out those lazy blighters of servants, will you, Bailey. I'll get a rope down to Tinker."

Bailey dashed across towards the servants godowns ready to kick them into wakefulness, while Blake ran across to where the galvanised bucket lay, and dragged it over to the edge of the well. He examined the rope critically. It was of twisted coir, and he did not know whether it would hold Tinker's weight or not. But just then it had to be risked, so he called down:

"Look out for the bucket coming down. Tinker. Hang on and use your toes and fingers against the sides as much as possible. I'll try and get you up that way."

A faint "all right" reached him, and then he lowered away the bucket. It took most of the rope to get it down, but at last he felt a tug as Tinker caught it; and again the lad's voice came up telling him to haul away.

Blake called down that he would wait for Bailey, for he knew the lad could not go under now, and just then Bailey, bearing another lantern, appeared. He set it down, and, as he took hold of the rope, said:

"Can't we understand it, Blake. There isn't a single dashed servant to be found in the place. They must have sneaked off for an all night *tamasha* after we went to bed. What do you suppose has happened— and that figure in the tree. Do you think it is really a man?"

"Don't know," panted Blake, pulling away. "The first thing is to get Tinker out while we can. If he gets a chill in there he will be down for a serious bout of it."

They drew away steadily, and, foot by foot, the rope came up through their hands. From time to time Tinker called that he was making it all right, and now his voice began to sound stronger. Still they kept at it, and once Blake's heart almost popped into his mouth as there came a sudden jerk on the rope, and it went flying through their hands as Tinker slipped and fell back.

But the lad succeeded in recovering himself on some obstruction in the side wall of the well, and once more came on. Up they got him until they could see him climbing, and, a few minutes later, he came near enough for them to reach him. They dragged him over the side where he lay prone, panting with exhaustion.

Blake bent over him in concern.

"Are you injured, my lad?" he asked.

"Don't think so," came the gasping reply. "Just about all in. Fell the whole way down, but luckily hit the water fair. Was about chilled to the bone. What became of the beggar who was on the roof?"

"Beggar on the roof! What do you mean?" asked Blake quickly.

"Native—prowling on the roof—tackled him in the tree—"

"Ah! We will attend to him. Can you manage to get upstairs?"

"Yes, sir!"

"Well, go at once. Get the flask in my room, and take a good stiff dose of spirit. Then give yourself a thorough rub down, and get into dry pyjamas. Don't lose a moment, or you will be in for a bad bout of fever. Get into bed when you have finished. I shall be up presently, and give you a dose of quinine. Take this lantern with you."

He helped Tinker to his feet, and, giving him the lantern, pushed him in the direction of the stairs. Tinker looked towards the tree, but the glare of the lantern hid what there was from him, and he kept on, for he was feeling so rotten he didn't care just then about anything else.

As soon as he was gone Blake and Bailey walked across and stood under the tree. While Bailey held the lantern Blake drew himself into the branches and began to climb. He went up easily enough, for the mohor was an easy tree, and then he came to what dangled there. He touched it, and then his fingers sought to find how the man was hanging. As he encountered the truth, he gave a low exclamation and slid down a few branches.

"Give me the lantern," he said. "I think the fellow is dead."

Bailey handed up the lantern and Blake climbed back. He held it close so he could make an examination, and then, as he saw how the native's head was caught, he turned and called down softly:

"It is a native—must be Tinker's roof prowler—he must have slipped in coming down, and his neck was caught between two branches. His own weight in plunging has hanged him as efficiently as it could have been done by a hangman. His neck is broken clean, and he must have died instantaneously. I'll get him clear and ease him down, Bailey."

He hung the lantern on a branch and managed to lift the body up so that he could slip the head out from the crotch of the branches where it had been caught. The body dragged heavily and limply in his grip, but he eased it from branch to branch until Bailey could reach up and catch hold. Then Blake took the lantern and came down, and between them they carried the lifeless form across to one of the servants' godowns, where they laid it on a charpoy.

Now, for the first time, Blake seemed to find time to attend to what Bailey had said about the servants not being visible.

"What was it you said?" he remarked. "Did you say there wasn't a single servant about the place?"

"That's it. Nary a smell of 'em. As I said, they have probably all gone off to some tamasha for the night."

"Umph. Maybe they have," remarked Blake. "Still, the cook didn't strike me as the sort who would go off on an all-night jamboree. He must he sixty-five if he is a day. Who sleeps in this godown?"

"The two mateys."

Blake picked up the lantern and swung it round.

"Do they keep their belongings in here?"

"Yes, what they have, which isn't much. I guess a shoestring would tie the lot in one bundle."

Blake made a tour of the place.

"Maybe it would," he replied when he came back, "but I can't see even that much, Bailey. Let us make a tour of the others."

Bailey wrinkled his brow as he digested Blake's remark, and followed the detective out of that godown and into the adjoining one.

"Who occupies this one?" asked Blake.

"The cook and the butler, I think. I have seen them both coming out of here."

"Well, they are the seniors and the most prosperous," remarked Blake. "Let's see what their belongings consist of."

They made a thorough examination of the place, but could find not a single scrap of anything that looked as if it might be the personal property of either the butler or the cook. Blake said nothing when they had finished; nor did Bailey. They entered another godown with the same result; and still a fourth which yielded nothing.

From there Blake led the way back to the compound and into the kitchen. Here the pots and pans were hung up in orderly array, and the ashes in the quaint little triple brick oven were still warm. But there was absolutely nothing that could have belonged to the cook or the cook's matey. Blake turned and looked at the engineer.

"They may have gone to an all-night tamasha," he said, with a grim smile, "but if you should ask me, Bailey, I should say that the whole caboodle of them have flown the coop. It is decidedly mysterious, and I should like to know just what connection their complete disappearance has with the native we found hanging in the tree. And that fellow is a person of some consequence among the natives. His clothes are not those of a servant. Let us go and see if Tinker can throw any light on the affair."

Followed by the dogs, who were now quiet enough, they mounted the stairs to Tinker's bath-room, and passed through into his bed-room. He had carried out orders and now lay ensconced beneath several heavy blankets which he had been wise enough to dig out and put on the bed despite the heat of the night.

Before questioning him, Blake got ten grains of quinine, which he made the lad swallow; then he said:

"If you don't feel up to it, my lad, we shall wait until the morning. But if you can manage, I'd like to know just what has been going on."

Tinker lifted himself up in bed, and, briefly, but leaving out no important detail, gave Blake a description of just what had happened from the moment when the spaniel had woke him to the time when, losing his grip, he had fallen through the branches of the mohor-tree and had plunged into the bottom of the well, more than thirty feet down.

Blake listened in silence; then he said:

"Did you see or hear anything of the servants?"

"No, guv'nor, I can't say I did. I don't remember that I did."

"Um! All right, my lad. You get to sleep. I'll come along presently to see if you are all right."

"Yes, I will, guv'nor. But what about that bird I tackled? Did he get away?"

"No. You might as well know the truth now, my lad. In slipping through the branches, you must have dragged him some of the way with you. At any rate, his feet certainly lost their hold, and he fell between two of the branches. His neck was caught in the crotch and was broken instantaneously just as if he had been hanged in the orthodox way. We don't know what he was doing about the place, but it must have been with some felonious intent in his mind. At any rate, he tried to murder you, so he has but paid a just penalty which Fate and no one else handed out to him. You were but an innocent instrument, so you needn't let that keep you awake."

"You bet I won't," said the lad. "He would have strangled me if he could, but, all the same, I am sorry the poor fool got his like that."

Blake nodded and left him, carrying the lantern with him. He found Bailey on the front veranda. He had lighted one of the petrol gas-lamps, and was pacing up and down with an expression of deep worry on his usually placid countenance. Blake set the lantern down and reached for the cigarettes.

"What do you make of it, Blake?" asked Bailey abruptly. "This sort of thing is beyond me. I have a feeling that something of a serious nature is afoot, or has been afoot, but it is beyond my grasp. I don't know India well enough. But you know it intimately. What is it all about?"

Blake tossed the end of the match over the railing and gazed out into the night. Just beneath his gaze, where the light from the lamp fell on it, he could see the blood red blossoms of a hibiscus-tree. It was standing there silent and sinister, as if symbolic of the lurking death which is forever abroad in that country of mystery. Then he turned back sharply.

"I can't answer your question, old man," he said quietly. "But I propose finding out. I am convinced that the servants have gone for good. They have taken all their belongings with them. And I am equally convinced that the man who was hanged in the mohor-tree

80

had something to do with their going. In my opinion, the first step is to identify that man. A native of good class does not spend his nights crawling about the roofs of European bungalows. That much is certain. What he wanted there, I don't know, but it will be daylight ere long, and then we shall make an examination. In the meantime, his death must be reported. The sub-inspector of police should be at his house now. One of us must walk down there and get him. Do you know where it is? Or would you rather stay here?"

"I'll do whichever you say. I don't know where the sub-inspector lives, but I can probably find it if you tell me the direction. I can knock up some native and ask him."

"No—not that. If it is all the same to you, I think I had better go. I shall not be long, and, in the meantime, you can remain on guard here. Incidentally, I don't for a moment think you will have any need for it, but I would suggest that you keep your pistol beside you."

"All right, I'll get it. What about you?"

"I shall take mine with me, and also, I think, the Airedale."

A few minutes later Blake was on his way, accompanied by Jock, the Airedale. He took the hurricane lantern, too, and, as he went out through the gates, set off at a brisk pace towards the main maidan, on the other side of which the sub-inspector lived. He passed the next compound, and then reached the corner of the maidan. Just as he turned it he thought he saw something moving ahead of him.

With the lantern swinging in front and at his side, the glare made it impossible for him to be sure, but he jerked the light behind him, and then he distinctly made out a moving mass some twenty or thirty yards in front.

He watched it, and then, as his eyes became more accustomed to the gloom, he saw that it was a rickshaw, and that the coolie between the shafts was running at top speed towards the other side of the maidan, where the club was situated.

Blake whistled at the fellow, but this only seemed to make him redouble his pace. Then Blake left the road and started on a run across the maidan with the intention of cutting off the fellow on the other side if he could.

But the coolie must have looked back and made out the lantern swinging over the grass, for he, too, left the road, and, since there was no obstruction, he was able to cut across the maidan, too. He passed the club flying, and then he swung round the other corner by the old

Dutch church (which is now the English church) and disappeared from view.

Blake drew up to a walk and abandoned the chase. But as he went along he was thinking over the odd incident, for odd it certainly was. It was a most unusual thing for a rickshaw coolie to be about the European quarter at that time of night, unless in the service of his master, who may have been down the backwater on business. And even if some chance had brought him along at such an hour, why had he fled on seeing a light? Even supposing he had taken out his master's rickshaw without authority, why should he run away when a light appeared?

Even if he had known it was an European coming along, he need not have been afraid; for, one rickshaw is so much like another, a passing European would not have been able to identify which vehicle it was. And he would have given little or no thought to the coolie, even if he had recognised him as the servant of another European.

Then why had the man fled so precipitately? He had been waiting for someone. Blake was certain of that. He had been lurking there in the shadows outside Spencer's stores, which had been closed since seven o'clock in the evening. Then for whom had he been waiting? Had he been waiting for someone who had not come —would now never come? Had he been waiting for the man whose neck had been broken in the mohor-tree?

It was just one more incident to add to the mystery of the night.

Blake kept on across the maidan, and, as far as he could see, there was no one but himself about. He passed the church, and strode along to the little triangular open space, which, with a mound in the middle of it, is all that marks the spot where the old Portuguese cathedral used to stand.

He passed the port office, and then took a turning to the right along a narrow street that was lined with small houses occupied by Eurasians. Before one of these he paused, and hammered on the door.

He got no answer the first time, but he persisted, and soon heard a sleepy voice inside asking what was wanted. He bent close and spoke curtly in English; and at the sound of the European voice the Eurasian sub-inspector scrambled out of bed and called that he was getting into his clothes.

Blake grew impatient waiting, but when the door finally opened, he saw the reason for the delay. The sub-inspector had taken time to get fully into his uniform. His dignity would not permit him to appear before an European in anything less.

He recognised Blake quickly enough, and saluted. He knew quite a lot about the famous English detective, and no small amount of thrills coursed through him every time Blake came to Cochin. He knew that Blake was a personal friend of Congrove sahib and Hitchcock sahib, and for that reason alone one to be greatly deferred to.

"I want you to come along with me, inspector," said Blake pleasantly. "Something has happened at the bungalow where I am staying that needs your attention. I will tell you about it as we go along."

The sub-inspector closed the door and stepped out beside Blake. As they went along, Blake said:

"Several curious things have happened, to be exact. In the first place, every one of the servants seems to have taken himself off, bag and baggage, while we were asleep. On top of that, my young assistant discovered a native prowling about on the roof of the bungalow and watched him until he came off the roof into a tree which grows close to the wall. That tree is just outside the room occupied by my assistant, and he swung himself out of the window and into the tree to tackle him. They fought among the branches, and, during the struggle, my assistant lost his foothold and fell. The native was not so fortunate. It appears that while he, too, was falling, his neck got caught between two of the branches and was broken. When we got him down, he was dead—I think he died instantaneously, for he was hanged as neatly as if he had been standing on a drop. You may know the native. I want you to have a look at him. And then we shall go into the affair in more detail. Perhaps you may be able to tell us what he was doing prowling about the roof."

"I don't know, sir, but I will do my best," answered the sub-inspector, and they said no more until they reached the bungalow. There Blake whistled up to Bailey, who joined them in the compound and all three went into the godown where the dead native was lying.

Blake held his lantern close so the sub-inspector could see plainly for his examination. He bent over the corpse, and, as he gazed upon the stiff features, he gave a low gasp of surprise. His face looked a little scared as he turned it up towards Blake.

"You recognise the fellow?" asked Blake sharply,

"Y-yes, sir, I do," he answered. "His name is Haridee Rathansey. He comes of a well-to-do family in the bazaar, and his uncle is the wealthiest dealer there."

"His name is it Bamjee Haridee?" asked Blake.

"Yes, sir, that is the uncle's name."

Blake shot a look at Bailey, who, however, seemed no further enlightened; then he said:

"Well, come upstairs, inspector. I shall make a statement now, and if you want me later I shall attend for the formalities."

He led the way to the front verandah, and seated himself at the desk. He mechanically wrote out a brief statement of what had happened, but all the time he was writing his mind was busy on the startling statement which the sub-inspector had made.

Haridee Rathansey! A nephew of Bamjee Haridee! That was the follow who had been prowling about the roof of the bungalow during the night. What would Bamjee Haridee say and do when he heard the news? That is what Blake was asking himself just then.

Now he was positive he was right in suspecting there had been some really deep purpose behind the whole thing. Bamjee Haridee's nephew did not come prowling about the roof of an European bungalow unless that were so. Had he been acting for Bamjee? If so, then it must have been a matter of some importance, or else Bamjee would have entrusted the job to a lesser agent.

Curious, Blake thought that, on the very night his theorising should point to the dealer, this thing should happen. Was it part and parcel of the mysterious occurrence that had swallowed up Green, the mycologist? Was Bamjee behind this and, if he was, then was there any connection between the fact that the schooner on which Tinker had seen Huxton Rymer and Mary Trent lay anchored just opposite Bamjee's mill jetty? Or was that sheer coincidence?

Blake rose and handed the statement to Bailey, asking him to witness it. Then, while he waited, he looked out over the veranda, and saw that the dawn was just showing through the morning mist which had come in from the backwater in the last half-hour. He took the paper and gave it to the sub-inspector, and, when the latter had read it and thrust it inside his tunic pocket, Blake said;

"The dawn is coming. Let us go into the compound, and see if we can discover what that fellow wanted on the roof."

He led the way and, on reaching the compound, they gathered in a little group just near the foot of the mohor-tree. Tinker had heard them, and, a few seconds later, his head appeared in the window. He saw in which direction their eyes were turned, and he, too, looked upwards towards the ridge of the roof. Thus they stood while the dawn grew and expanded across the sky, and then, silhouetted against the lightening grey, they could make out something small and of uneven form on the tip of the ridge.

They still stood looking, and then suddenly Blake saw what it was. As he made it out he struck his thigh impatiently and said:

"Why the deuce didn't I guess that before? Of course it is that! It couldn't be anything else." And the sub-inspector nodded his agreement, while Bailey looked blanker than ever.

What they saw was a small barred owl.

CHAPTER 13.   The Tabu on Blake's Bungalow—Compelled to Quit Cochin.

"WHAT does it mean?" asked Bailey.

"I'll tell you later," answered Blake. "The first thing to do is to get it down if possible before it is seen. One of us will have to go up and get it. I fancy we shall find it is not free to move very far."

Bailey started for the tree.

"I'll get it," he announced. "You have been doing everything to-night. It is up to me do take a hand for a change."

Blake did not raise any objection. The engineer was a small, wiry man, very active, and he proved, a few minutes later, an expert climber. He made his way up through the mohor tree, and swung from there on to the roof of the back veranda. The slope was easy enough, and they watched him while he went up hand over hand to the ridge of the roof.

He had just reached it, and was on the point of putting out his hand to clutch the owl when he happened to look over the roof to the road in front of the bungalow, and the next second he had dodged down again. He turned and looked down at Blake.

"Did you say it was important to get this thing down before it was seen?" he asked, in a low tone.

Blake nodded, a little puzzled.

"Well, take a look through the arch to the road," added the engineer. "It looks as if half the natives in the place were out there."

Blake took a few steps to the right, so he could look through the passage that ran under the centre of the house to the front gates. And then he saw what Bailey meant.

Out in the little maidan that lay in front of the house, and between it and the bungalow which was used by the English padre on his occasional visits to the station, he saw a thick mass of white-clad natives. They were packed closely together, and each and every one had his eyes glued up towards the roof of the bungalow.

They were as silent as if some mystic command lay upon them, and it was just because of that silence Blake had not spotted them before. Usually, any gathering of natives, from two upwards, is about the noisiest thing imaginable, unless it be a collection of Indian crows.

And what he saw was enough to tell him the damage was done; that what he had been trying to avoid was already accomplished. How they had collected there in such numbers and in such silence was a mystery; but they were there plain enough, and must have gathered just as dawn began to break, or immediately after he had looked over the front verandah before coming down into the compound. Which means that his suspicions were now confirmed.

He stepped back and made a sign to Bailey.

"It doesn't matter now." he said. "But bring the bird down, and take care you don't injure it. That would only make matters worse—if it is possible."

Bailey raised himself, and, in full view of the crowd in the road, caught hold of the owl. The little creature struggled fiercely in his hand, but he dragged it away from where it clung, and as he did so muttered to himself:

"Clipped wings and bird lime! So that was how it was stuck here! Now I wonder what that part of it means?"

Holding the owl carefully, he slid back down the roof and climbed through the branches of the mohor tree to the ground. As he held out the bird Sexton Blake also saw how its escape from where it had been placed had been guarded against. Not only had its wings been clipped, but the bottoms of its feet had been thickly smeared with bird lime, and now Blake knew he was wondering just what his duty called upon him to do. But Blake was determined that he should do nothing precipitate.

"I want you to remain here for now," he said curtly. "You and I know what this owl means. Now that it is gone, and they all know it actually was on the roof, they will soon take themselves off. But they can't yet know that the man who put it on the roof is dead, and I don't want that news to leak through to the bazaar yet. Let us go back upstairs again. I shall place the owl here in the tree for the time being. It has done all the damage it can. Come along, Bailey, and I will explain."

Blake motioned for them to be seated in the living-room while he walked out on to the veranda and looked at the crowd. He could see that they were already on the move, so, with a shrug, he returned to the living-room, where he saw Tinker had arrived. He lit a cigarette and seated himself.

"The position is just this, Bailey. That owl which was placed on the roof during the night is, to the natives, a symbol of tabu. In fact, it is quite the strongest form of tabu which they possess. Am I right, inspector?"

"Yes, sir."

"It is not only a tabu on the house, but on the occupants as well," proceeded Blake. "There is no doubt in my mind now that Haridee Rathansey came here last night for the express purpose of placing this house, and those in it, out of bounds utterly, so to speak. That in itself would explain why all the servants decamped, bag and baggage.

"Now, the point is just whom was it aimed at? I think I can answer that. I have private reasons for my opinion. I think it was aimed at me and Tinker, and not at you. But while we remain, here, you will be under the ban as well. So we must make a move."

"Under the ban! Make a move!" snorted Bailey. "Do you think that tomfoolery cuts any ice with me? Let them keep on at their monkey tricks if it does them any good. Do you think I am going to let that bunch of yahoos scare me with a harmless little owl?"

Blake made a negative gesture.

"You miss the point. It is not tomfoolery, as you will soon discover. It isn't the owl—it is what it stands for. There isn't a native who will come near the place until the tabu is removed, and the only person who can remove it is the one who originated it; and I think I could name that person. It is the most unlucky symbol there is. That owl means all sorts of dire things to the natives, which we can scarcely grasp. But it is a very serious reality, as you will find out.

"While that tabu remains, you won't be able to get a single soul to come near the bungalow. You won't be able to buy a scrap of food in the bazaar. You won't get a rickshaw man or a munji man to take you about. You won't be able to go and stay at the club either, for the moment you did so, the boys there would leave in a body. It is just as complete as it can possibly be, and you must understand that. When I say 'you' I mean Tinker and myself as well. In fact, I particularly mean us. Once we are out of it I think you will find the tabu removed from you."

"But—but I don't understand, Blake. Why should this be done to you?"

"It is part and parcel of what I was telling you about last night," answered Blake evasively. "What we have to do now is to make our plans without delay. Every second counts."

The sub-inspector hadn't the faintest idea what Blake was talking about, but he tried to look wise, and nodded his head from time to time as Blake talked. Suddenly the detective turned to him, and shot out a question.

"I don't think it can be known yet that Haridee Rathansey is dead," he said. "Do you?"

"No, sir—no, Mr. Blake, not if it happened after the servants left."

"Well, it did. Now then, I have an idea he came in a rickshaw, and I fancy the rickshaw man is back in the bazaar by now. But they can't know anything definite as yet. But Bamjee Haridee won't be long in making inquiries, and, besides, there is another thing to think of. The body must be handed over for burial soon. It won't keep long in this climate. But what I want to know from you, inspector, is, how long do you think you can keep the news from Bamjee Haridee? This is important."

"Why, sir, I will do as you wish about it, but it won't be possible to conceal it many hours."

"Quite so. Do you think you can keep the news quiet until some time this afternoon?"

"Yes, sir, I could manage that. But Bamjee Haridee is a powerful man in the bazaar, sir, and he will be very angry."

Blake leant forward and wagged a stern finger at the chicken-hearted Eurasian.

"He won't be one quarter as angry as I shall be, if it leaks out before this afternoon" he said. "Nor one tenth as angry as Congrove sahib will be. Your duty is to your department, inspector, and don't you let any rich bazaar dealer scare you. I'll settle him if he tries that."

"I'll do whatever you say, sir."

"That's the ticket. Now then, this is what you have to do. You remain here at the bungalow with Bailey sahib until this afternoon. I and my assistant will leave Cochin. In view of what has happened, it is useless for us to remain longer. I shall have to approach the business that brought me here from another angle. That will free you, Bailey, and enable you to get on with your work. On my way to the jetty I shall step in at Phillips' office, and also see Craven, and tell them what has happened. I think you will find that they will come and see you at once, and by the time the body is removed the tabu should be removed.

"For ourselves, it will be useless to try and get any native to do anything for us. We shall have to fend for ourselves. How are you feeling now, Tinker?"

"As right as rain, guv'nor."

"Good. Then here is your job. I shall write out a list now, which you will take round the corner to Spencer's stores. The Eurasian in charge there dare not refuse to serve you. You will buy what I put on the list, and bring it round here yourself. Then we shall make a couple of packs and get away. We shall have to get hold of a munji and paddle ourselves across the backwater, and if we get a move on we shall be in time to get to Ernakulam before the morning train leaves."

"Then you are determined to go?" asked Bailey.

"I am determined to leave Cochin," answered Blake firmly. "This tabu has put a crimp in my business, so what is the use of remaining? Another time, perhaps, 1 shall come back."

And at that moment Bailey was wondering to himself why the man of whom he had heard so much, the sleuth of whom it had been said that he never left a trail until he got his man, should be driven from the place so easily.

The sub-inspector was not thinking that, but he was figuring to himself that, with Blake and Tinker gone, he would find it less difficult to explain matters to Bamjee Haridee, of whom, despite what Blake said, he was in deadly fear. And why shouldn't he be? Hadn't the dealer, for some reason of his own, put the tabu of the owl on the bungalow where Blake was staying, and hadn't it succeeded in its purpose?

That was enough for the sub-inspector, for, after all, he had a great quantity of native blood in him, and while he was a professed Christian, he still had in his make-up all the fantastic superstition of the native.

And, having started Bailey on one line of thought and the sub-inspector on another, Sexton Blake shot a quick look at Tinker, and in that flash Tinker knew, as well as if Blake had told him aloud, that he had done exactly what he had set out to do.

Soon after that Tinker got into his clothes and took Blake's list round to the stores not far away. The sub-inspector went down to see to certain things about the body, and Bailey walked up and down in a worried way while Blake attended to preparations for his and Tinker's departure.

By the time Tinker had returned with most of the things Blake had specified on the list Blake was ready, and it did not take those two experienced campaigners long to get their packs completed. Bailey wanted to come along with them and help to paddle the munji over the backwater; but Blake would not permit it.

"You can't get ahead with your work until the tabu is removed," he said. "And it will need Phillips, or Craven, or both of them, to help you in that. But one thing I want to take up with you before I go. It is altogether likely that Bamjee Haridee, the uncle of the dead man, will appear on the scene. He may try and question you, but I want you to say just as little as possible. You can tell him that a statement has already been made and handed to the inspector, and that you were not a witness of the accident which caused his nephew's death; nor did you know anything about it until it was all over. That lets you out completely, and that is the way I want it."

Bailey promised that he would follow instructions; and a few minutes later Blake and Tinker, with their packs on their backs, started out on foot for the jetties. As they went along they caught more than one native eyeing them surreptitiously, but they paid no attention, although Blake knew that, by the time they reached the jetty, it would be known in the bazaar that they had left the bungalow, bound for some unknown destination.

On the way along they stopped first at Phillips' office, and then at Craven's, where Blake explained as much as was necessary of what had occurred. Of course, neither of the European merchants knew why Blake was in Cochin; nor could they guess why the tabu of the owl had been placed on the bungalow.

Blake simply said that it was aimed at him and that, once he had departed, he thought it could be removed from Bailey; that he had an idea the sub-inspector thought Bamjee Haridee was the man to see about having it removed. They both promised to do what they could; and both insisted, too, that one of their boats should take the pair across the backwater, being manned by Eurasians. But Blake refused these offers.

On leaving Craven's office, they made for the public jetty, which was only a short distance away. Lying there were several munjis of various sizes, and, standing at the end of the jetty, Blake deliberately picked out one of the largest and most serviceable-looking of the lot. He coolly entered this, and Tinker followed.

Several natives who were lounging in the shadow of the wall of the coir yarn press regarded them with some interest, and, indeed, the owner of that same munji was one of the group.

But not a word of protest was raised as the two Europeans pushed off, and, each with a paddle, sent the light craft flying out into the backwater.

They paddled along past the custom-house jetty, and then shot over in a north-easterly direction, heading for the upper part of Ernakulam where the narrow gauge line which connected with the main South Indian line at Shoranur sixty miles away, had its terminus.

On the way they passed Candle Island, a small backwater island occupied by the godowns of one of the big merchant firms, and then they slid past the point of Bolghatty Island, a bit of coco-nut covered land a few hundred yards wide, and about two miles long.

On the lower end of this, past which they were going, was the British Residency, its well-kept lawns and heavily-foliaged trees looking most inviting after the eternal coco-nuts.

At the time the resident was away, as Blake knew. Had he been at the residency Blake might have adopted a different plan.

Once past the point of Bolghatty, they swung round sharply to the left and paddled past the new coco-nut-oil mill which had been erected not long before by an Indian firm, and which, in fact, had been the inspiration to the soap company in England to think of doing the same. It was idle then, however, for there were not enough nuts coming in to keep the oil presses busy.

Past this mill they turned into a short canal on the right, and, at the end of this they reached a small float which was moored to the bank just opposite the railway station.

They stepped out there, tied the munji and left it for its owner to retrieve as best he might. They knew that gossip would soon inform him where it had been left.

Then they made for the station, where Blake bought two first-class tickets tor Shoranur. He was glad that they seemed to be the only Europeans travelling up by the morning train, for it meant they could have a compartment all to themselves, which was what he had been hoping.

They got in at once, and Blake took the precaution to bolt the door against intrusion. Then while the hordes of natives bustled, and jammed and chattered on the platform until the very last minute, he explained to Tinker what he planned doing.

Tinker grinned as he listened. He had not had the faintest fear that Blake was allowing Bamjee Haridee to drive him out of the place; but he had been no end intrigued to know just what Blake was up to. And now as he knew, he wrinkled his brow and, after a few moments, said:

"There is a place just about half-way along to Alwaye, guv'nor. That would be about seven miles. Do you remember that, on the right as we are travelling, there is a black laterite hill? There is quite a grade near there, and a tunnel at the top. If we could manage it there, we shouldn't be seen from the train."

"You have picked on the very spot on which I had fixed, my lad," rejoined Blake. "We shall make the attempt there."

And then they sat in silence while the train rattled on, swaying so violently at times that it seemed as if they must go flying off the rails. But the wheels clung in some miraculous manner, and at last Blake gave a sign to Tinker.

"About, another mile," he said; and the lad understood.

They swung on their packs and made for the door opposite the one by which they had entered the compartment. Blake opened it a trifle, and then they stood while the train gradually slowed down as they took the grade to which Tinker had referred. They could hear the engine making a great labour of it, and then, peering out, Blake could see the mouth of the tunnel at the top.

"I'll go first," he said. "Mind how you jump. And the minute you hit the ground, flatten yourself against the wall until the train gets past."

He opened the door wider then; the next instant they were puffing into the tunnel. Blake watched his chance and swung down. He was immediately swallowed up in the thick smoke that was sweeping back through the tunnel, and into this pall Tinker plunged a second or two later.

He flattened himself against the wall as Blake had told him to do, and then, when the last coach had gone lumbering past, he started on towards where he knew the opening to be situated, coughing and half-choked with the noxious fumes which were filling the place.

On reaching the open-air he inhaled gratefully, and then found Blake doing the same. They waited a few minutes to get the gas out of their lungs; then Blake started on and, leaving the railway, took into the cover of the thick woods which grew almost up to the edge of the right of way.

Blake kept the railway track in view as a guide, however, and as they had the whole day ahead of them they took it easy.

They covered a couple of miles or so until they came to a small stream, and here Blake pulled up.

"Might as well have chota here," he remarked. "We don't want to hit Ernakulam again before dark."

So they took it easy; it was not until the sun was low in the west, and the heat of early afternoon had lessened that they started on again.

It was just getting dusk when they reached the edge of the backwater above Ernakulam, and here the coco-nuts grew so thickly they could see scarcely twenty yards ahead of them.

Blake struck for the very edge of the water, and then slumped along through the mud until he came upon what he was seeking, and what he knew he would find easily enough sooner or later. It was a small munji, and the paddles were in it.

He motioned for Tinker to get in, then he did likewise, and they drove the munji out into the backwater. It was now full dusk, and they knew it was most unlikely they would be seen by anyone, except some stray fishermen on their way home.

They had embarked just opposite the upper part of Bolghatty Island, at the other extreme of which the residency was situated, and they steered a course that took them round the upper end. They pulled on close to the western shore of the island here, and paddled softly along until they had almost reached the boundary line of the residency grounds.

There Blake drove the nose into the mud, and they drew the munji up until it was completely concealed from view from the backwater.

Then Blake led the way as one certain of his direction, and it was only a few minutes before he came out before a small, but sturdily built, native bamboo and palm-thatched hut.

"Here we are, my lad," he said cheerfully. "I don't think there is a soul living on the whole island except the caretaking servants at the residency. I remember this little hut from the last time we were here. Some of the Resident's junglies used to stay in it—they wouldn't mix with the other servants, and for that reason we should be fairly safe from being molested. The servants will have it under a tabu, too, I imagine, after it has been occupied by junglies.

"Now, off with your pack, and let us get one of the candles lit inside. We daren't risk a fire yet. But before I finish with us, we shall be able to move as openly as we desire."

Thus was it that Blake "fled" from the station as Bamjee Haridee had intended that he should.

CHAPTER 14.   The Intercepted Letter—Bamjee Haridee Plays a Strong Hand.

MARY TRENT was feeling happier. That morning early she had another talk with Rymer about Bamjee Haridee, and had wrung a promise from him that, after just one more division, he would throw up the game and clear out.

Mary couldn't have told herself why she was so anxious for Rymer to break with the dealer. It was one of those strange feminine intuitions that somehow she knew was right, and yet couldn't analyse.

Rymer had more than a little faith in the girl's judgment, for he had seen her in too many tight corners in the past not to have a very great respect for her brains and finesse. But on this occasion he thought she was getting panicky over nothing. He put it down to the heat and boredom of the place, and let it go at that.

But if she was so keen on getting out with what they had, why, he figured, there was no reason to refuse her. They had a pretty good haul, anyway.

He didn't expect to see the dealer again before evening, so they took things easy during the day. If he had known what had been going on during the night he would have been more anxious to hear what Bamjee had to say. But he knew nothing of what had taken place, so did not concern himself with looking up Bamjee. He knew that the dealer would show up by the evening at the latest.

After tiffin Rymer stretched out in a deck chair beneath the double canvas over the poop, and read drowsily for a bit before dropping into a siesta. Not so Mary. She had been busy checking up their stores in preparation for departure, and then she made ready to go ashore. While Rymer slept she went below, and was down there a considerable time.

When she again came on deck she was dressed in a fresh white muslin frock, with a tricky little white straw hat to match, and was carrying a gaily-coloured Japanese sunshade. She tripped aft and touched Rymer on the shoulder. As he came awake with a snort, she said:

"If we are going away to-morrow or next day, there are some stores I must order. I want to go to the club, and see if the club butler can let me have some ice for to-morrow. I want to get there and away before any of the members turn up for tennis. And while I am there, I want to get something in the bazaar to send as a souvenir to Anna Thurston."

Anna Thurston was Zulaika, the clairvoyant, who had worked with Rymer and Mary Trent on several occasions.

"All right," said Rymer sleepily. "But I could look after the stores."

"No, I'll get them," she responded.

She walked to the rail and waved her parasol towards one of the bazaar jetties. The munji man whom she had been using of late saw her and came at once. Mary stepped in, and was soon on the jetty. She got a rickshaw there, and told the coolie to go along through the bazaar until she told him to stop.

She had him pull up in front of one of the shops, which she entered in order to select the gift for Anna Thurston. After some deliberation, she chose a sandalwood box, which had been hand-carved and decorated with ivory.

She also secured a piece of strong paper and some twine, and with her purchases returned to the rickshaw.

Her next call was at the club, and as it was still mid-afternoon, she ran no risk of meeting any of the members. In fact, the "boys" were just coming on duty, and she had to wait some minutes before the butler showed up. She tipped him, as usual, and ordered some ice for the following day. The ice had to come five hundred miles across country from Madras.

Then she drove to Spencers, where she left her list of stores, which she instructed should be sent to the schooner, and as she had been a most profitable customer during her stay, the Eurasian clerk was only too glad to do so.

That done, she re-entered the rickshaw, and told the coolie to drive on round the point to the lighthouse on the sea side. She got out here, told the man to wait, and tripped across the sand dunes to the beach, where she found a secluded spot in the shade of the old bastion.

She settled down there, and from her bag took a letter which she had already written to Zulaika. She placed this inside the sandalwood box, and filled the rest of the space with what looked like a wad of crushed tissue paper.

Then she closed the box, and proceeded to wrap it up. When it was tied to her satisfaction, she sealed it with some wax, she also took from her bag. Then she addressed it to Anna Thurston at her London address. When she had finished she smoked a cigarette, and then re-entered the rickshaw.

She ordered the man to drive to the post office, where she posted her box by registered post. Following that, she drove down the beach road for the change of air and view, and it was getting on for dusk when the rickshaw man at last started back through the Fort.

She had just passed the club, where some of the European ladies on the station and some of the men were playing their daily game of tennis when, as the rickshaw rounded the bend by the church, she saw a short, comfortable-looking European lady just ahead of her.

This lady turned as she approached, and as she saw Mary, she lifted her hand. The rickshaw coolie stopped, and the woman, whom Mary knew to be the port officer's wife, said:

"You are the lady who is staying on the schooner down the backwater, aren't you!"

Mary acknowledged that she was, and the other went on:

"I have seen you pass several times. I am sure you must find it lonely all by yourself. If you had left cards at the club, it would have been more pleasant for you. But won't you come along home with me, and have tea? Perhaps you would stay to dinner, too?"

Mary stepped out of the rickshaw and joined the good soul. She had had her own reason for not going to the club, and had they been remaining longer, she would have refused the well-meant invitation. But as they were leaving the following day, or the next, she saw no reason why she should not accept the invitation, which she did, and, it must be confessed, gratefully.

So they walked on to the Port Office and up to the wide upstairs veranda, where, tea was served. The genial port officer joined them there, and the upshot was that he insisted that he should send a note to "her husband" —whom he knew as Captain Palmer—and ask him to come to dinner. Mary yielded, and the port officer went down to send the note.

Little did Mary dream what was to happen to that note before it reached Rymer; nor just how the chance invitation from the port officer's wife was to fit in neatly with the schemes of another person.

The port officer despatched the note by Mary's rickshaw man. He wanted to send one of his own office peons, but she would not permit it. Then she made herself as charming as could be, although she steered wide of any reference to what she and Rymer were doing in the place.

•　　•　　•　　•　　•

The rickshaw coolie took the note, left his rickshaw under the port office veranda, and started off at a trot through the bazaar. He had no other intention than to do as he had been instructed, but he was not destined to reach the jetty without being intercepted; and this is how it came about.

Early that afternoon Bamjee Haridee discovered what had happened to his nephew. Now, whatever the dealer's faults might have been, he was possessed of one great virtue, and that was a tremendous fondness for his family and relatives. It is, as a matter of fact, a very common virtue among the Indians.

It was the sub-inspector who, filled with funk, broke the news to Bamjee. The dealer heard him out; then he waved him from the place and closed the door of his private office.

His grief was profound. He sat rocking back and forth in a paroxysm of wailing which could be heard in the outer premises, and which caused his clerks to steal about in silent dread.

They all knew, the whole bazaar knew, that Haridee Rathansey had been the apple of Bamjee's eye, the pomegranate in his garden.

Bamjee had no sons of his own, and his nephew was to have been his heir. He had watched him grow to manhood with an eye of pride and love. And now! It was all gone—wiped out as if it had never been.

He could not believe it. He could not conceive that he, Bamjee, had been made to suffer this thing. Nor did he pause to remember that it was due to his own subtle schemes that this retribution had recoiled upon him.

When the first paroxysm had passed he walked out on to the small jetty at the back of his bazaar godown, and seating himself there, gave himself up to thought. As he gazed down the backwater his eyes rested on the white schooner, and he gave a snarl as he remembered that if it had not been for the man on that schooner, his nephew would still be alive.

He had been thinking a good deal about Rymer during the past few days, and his thoughts must have communicated themselves in some clairvoyant manner to Mary Trent, for Bamjee had been planning to do just what Mary had feared.

He had been laying his plans to "double cross" Rymer, though, up to then, he had not figured out exactly how he would do it. While he sat there he saw the munji slip across from the jetty, and saw Mary Trent step in. He frowned. He knew that the white woman did not like him, and he would have liked to have hit out at her if he could. But that chance might come yet, he figured.

The thing to do was to hit on some plan which could be carried out without delay. He had still to get certain particulars of the affair at the bungalow the previous night, but one thing was certain —his nephew had met his death through the man, Sexton Blake. That man must die.

Then, too, there was still the other white man at his own house by the mill. He must be dealt with, too. How could all this be brought together, as it were, in order that he could make a clean sweep of all of them.

Could he play off one against the other so that he, Bamjee, should take all the profit, and none of the risk? He set his subtle Eastern mind to work, and for the better part of an hour he sat in deep thought.

He knew that Blake and his assistant had left Cochin that morning, and the sub-inspector had told him they had taken the train from Ernakulam, and Bamjee had lost no time in sending a trusted clerk across the backwater to find out if this was so; and to send telegrams to agents of his along the line to get track of them and discover whither they were bound.

If they kept on to Madras, then they were out of his reach, and he would have to satisfy his vengeance with what he could do to Rymer and the mycologist.

It was just then that this same clerk came out on the jetty to find him. He had just returned from Ernakulam, and he had some strange things to tell Bamjee.

Bamjee listened in silence, and then, suddenly, he saw his way clear. He rose and hurried back into his office. He sent one of his clerks over the backwater again in order to supplement the report he had just received.

He sent another through to the European quarter to get further information there. And still a third he instructed to go to the jetty opposite the schooner in order to keep watch there.

And, finally, he set himself to solve the one remaining difficulty—how to keep Mary Trent out of the way for that evening.

He knew she had gone up to the Fort, and he had not seen her return. But she might have come back while he had been sitting out on his jetty, although he had not seen the munji return to the schooner. He was in his front shop, sunk in thought, trying to get round this difficulty, when he spied the coolie whom he knew usually pulled her about in his rickshaw, trotting through the bazaar without his vehicle, and with a white envelope in his hand.

Bamjee made a peremptory gesture for the coolie to stop, and his word was law to any coolie. The man came obediently, and Bamjee questioned him curtly. The coolie told him all he knew—where he had taken the white memsahib, and that he had left her at the port office.

Bamjee took the letter and read the superscription. Then he went into his back room and put some water on to boil. In a few minutes the steam was rising, and he had little difficulty in steaming open the flap of the envelope. It is difficult enough at any time in that moist climate to get an envelope to stick.

He read what the port officer had written to Rymer, and, as he finished, he nodded his head slowly. He couldn't have asked for anything better. He put the letter back in the envelope, and re-sealed it. Then he gave it to the coolie, and told him to take it on as he had been instructed.

As soon as the man had trotted on, Bamjee called for his rickshaw and drove through his own mill jetty. He entered his motor-boat there and crossed to the schooner. He reached the deck while Rymer was reading the note from the port officer, and Bamjee waited until he had finished. Then, before Rymer could write a reply, the dealer said:

"Will you walk to the stern with me, please? I have very important things to discuss with you."

Rymer did so, and then the dealer, adopting a tone of deep sorrow, told him what had happened to his nephew. Rymer sympathised with him, for he knew that the old rascal had been really fond of the youth. But he knew there was something else to come. And he was not mistaken.

"You were right," Bamjee said, after a pause. "This man, Sexton Blake, came here to discover what he could about the nuts. I did what I could to deal with him because he was our enemy. I have given the life of the one I loved most in order to please you. And now you must do something in return. As for the man who is a prisoner in my house, I shall deal with him later. He is a fool, but they must pay for the life of my nephew."

"You would be a fool yourself to do any harm to the man whom you hold prisoner," said Rymer. "He is a government man, Bamjee, and if it was traced to you, you would find yourself in a very bad position. I am willing to do what I can. In fact, I wanted to tell you that after to-night's division I should do no more. I have enough, and I want to get away. But I am willing to do what I can before I go. I know how you feel, and I sympathise with you. Don't think I should not take great pleasure in striking at this man Sexton Blake, if I had the chance. I should have done so, had you not felt so sure that you could 'fix' him. But he does not 'fix' as easily as that. Yet you say he left Cochin, so, if he is gone away, what can I do?"

"He left Cochin, but—he has returned," said the dealer slowly. "'Listen. He is cunning, is that man. He left with the young one this morning. They bought stores and went on foot. They took a munji at the public jetty, and allowed it to be known that they were going away. They even took the train to Ernakulam; their tickets were purchased for Shoranur. But they did not even arrive at Alwaye!"

"What the devil do you mean?" asked Rymer quickly.

"My clerk found out. They jumped out of the train before it got to Alwaye. There is one place where they could do so. They kept to the cover of the woods all day, but they were seen in the neighbourhood of Ernakulam just about two hours ago. They stole a munji there, and went across to Bolghatty. There is a hut there—they are in that. So they have not left; and it means that this man, Sexton Blake, is, as I have said, a cunning one. He is still looking to find what he can. I have sent another man to watch them. He will return soon to report, and you shall see that I speak the truth."

Rymer brought his hand down hard, "By heavens!" he cried. "If that is so, just let me get at him! I shall show you whether he can be handled or not! I swear that before I leave here I shall 'fix' Sexton Blake, if it is the last thing I do."

And Bamjee smiled under cover of the dusk. And well he might, for Rymer had spoken just as he had hoped. He might have spoken differently had Mary Trent been there. But she wasn't; nor would he see her until after he had carried out the plans which he and Bamjee settled then and there, for, a little later, the rickshaw coolie was sent back to the port office with a note saying that Rymer regretted that business should prevent him from going to the port office for dinner, but insisting that Mary should remain.

He asked that the port officer should send one of his peons with her when she returned, to see her safely through the bazaar; and then, while Bamjee went ashore to get together the men who would be necessary for the job which was afoot, Rymer ate a hurried dinner.

CHAPTER 15.   Sexton Blake's Plan of Action—Rymer Forces Matters—The Death Struggle.

BEFORE sending Tinker to the stores to get the different items he had written down, Sexton Blake had figured out, more or less, just what he intended doing. Therefore, he had included several items which Tinker had found rather mystifying, but which, once Blake set to work on the island, he soon understood the meaning of.

Blake set out the various necessary items, and then the pair of them proceeded to strip. From head to foot they stained their bodies from a tin of stain which was among the items purchased, and, following that, they draped themselves in loin cloths, short dhooties, and round their heads, wrapped common bits of cotton cloth like any coolie would wear.

It was not a sufficiently complete disguise to do duty during the glare of the day, but it would pass well enough at night, and serve for the purpose Blake had in view.

He had been giving a good deal of thought to the whole problem ever since he had made the startling discovery of the pearls in the diseased coco-nuts, and, in doing so, he had linked up Bamjee Haridee with the plot. What had happened in the night had but confirmed him in that suspicion, and it wasn't a very long jump from that to the point where he could see half a dozen things which pointed to Huxton Rymer being mixed up with the dealer.

Blake knew his native well enough to realise that Bamjee would never take the death of his relative lying down. He might or might not believe that it had been an accident, but that would not make any difference. He would be out hotfoot for vengeance, and Blake knew it.

That was one reason why Blake had pretended to leave Cochin. But he did not know that the sub-inspector would tell Bamjee about his nephew's death as early in the day as he had. Nor did he dream that Bamjee had at once sent a man to trail them. That was one of those things which no man could have foreseen.

Blake had been thinking about Green, the mycologist, too. He had said very little to Phillips and Craven that morning, for he still wished to keep his connection with the business a secret if possible. But he was not forgetting the theory he had formed.

He was determined first to solve the mystery of how the nuts

104

were infected, and then he would search for the missing mycologist.

Now it seemed perfectly certain to Blake that the infection of the nuts was being carried out deliberately, and he could only figure one way how that could he done— by inoculation. It was that which made his mind look towards Rymer, so to say, for he knew Rymer was no mean scientist, and in such a plot would be right in his element.

Blake realised that, if he was right, then the work could only be done in the most surreptitious manner—which was enough to say that the plotters would be most likely to carry it out under cover of night when there was no one about the topes.

Blake knew that the evil spirits which every coolie believed to be abroad after dark would be sufficient to guarantee that the topes would be deserted after sundown, and that the plotter's could work unmolested and unseen.

It was on that basis he was building. And it was for that reason he had adopted the disguise of a coolie for himself and Tinker. That evening he intended taking the munji, and planned that he and the lad would make a slow tour of as much of the backwater as possible in order to see if they could come upon anything.

Once he could get some confirmation that his theory was sound, Blake would soon figure out a way of dealing with the marauders so as to make a complete cleanup in one raid.

But others were working as fast as he, and he was to discover that before the night was very old. When he was satisfied that their disguise would pass muster, Blake and the lad got something to eat; then they sat and waited until it was close on ten o'clock.

"Time to be making a move," said Blake, then in a low tone: "We'll push along down towards Vendurthy first, and make a tour of each side of the backwater there. We'll stick close to the shore, and just keep the munji barely moving. If you ever used a paddle silently in your life, my lad, see that you do so even more silently to-night. One little breath of suspicion, and the game will be all up."

"I'll—" Tinker started to reply, then suddenly he leant over and clutched Blake's arm.

"Out there, guv'nor," he whispered. "Isn't that a boat? Yes, and there is another and a third. Jinks, guv'nor, they seem to be coming straight on here."

Blake peered out towards the three blotches which the lad had spotted. Just then there was a flash of phosphorescence close to one of them, and he knew a paddle had come out of the water. He turned swiftly.

"Stay here," he whispered. "You are right. I'll get the pistols from the hut."

He was away like a snake, and Tinker sat motionless in the shadow watching while the three dark blotches came nearer and nearer. Blake was back then without the lad having heard him, and his fingers closed mechanically on the weapon which Blake pushed into his hand.

"On your feet," said Blake. "Get in here behind the trees. They are coming here right enough. I'll make sure before I hail them. There is something wrong, and it looks like an attack to me."

They took cover a little further back, and then, as it became plain that the three boats were coming into the bank, Blake gave a hail in Mallayalee. The next moment his suspicions were only too well confirmed when a voice answered, speaking mockingly in English; and he knew it was Huxton Rymer.

"It's all right, Blake," said the voice. "We are coming ashore. It will be better for you to make no fuss, for we are too many for you. Three boats here with six men in each boat, besides myself. And there are another four boats watching the island at different points, so you can't escape."

"All right, Rymer," answered Blake. "Come on and see how far you get with it. I hope Miss Trent isn't with you, because we shall not hold our fire."

"You needn't worry—she isn't here," replied Rymer.

"Is your friend Bamjee Haridee with you?" called Blake.

Rymer laughed as the nose of the boat almost touched the mud.

"Bamjee will attend to what I leave of you," he said. "At present he is mourning the death of his nephew. A sad case that. So I am handling matters for him. So on guard, Sexton Blake. I'm going to 'get' you this time."

As he spoke Rymer leapt ashore, and the coolies from all three boats swarmed after him. Rymer came crashing on, and then levelling his pistol he sent a bullet crashing towards the spot from which Blake's voice had come.

But Blake and Tinker were not there. They had shifted over behind another tree, and no sooner had Rymer's weapon crashed out than Blake and Tinker both shot. Blake aimed at the place where he had seen the flash while Tinker shot bang into the mob of natives. There was a yell as one of the coolies went down, and then, at a word from Rymer, they came on.

Blake knew they must do quick execution if they were to have the slightest chance of edging out of this trap. Therefore he shot out a command to Tinker to make every bullet tell, and their heavy automatics literally sprayed lead into the closely-packed mob as it came on. One and two, and another and another, went down under the heavy impact of the bullets.

But with Rymer urging them, they came on again; and then, while Blake tried to stem the tide with his last two cartridges, Tinker dropped back to slip in a fresh clip. The lad rushed out to take up the defence, and, before Blake could reload, Rymer was in on him. Blake forgot all about the natives then; he knew only one thing— that at last he was at hand-grips with Rymer, and that there and then the thing must be settled.

They crashed terrifically, and, as if by mutual consent, neither attempted to use his weapon. In fact, Blake's dropped to the ground, and he was only vaguely aware that Tinker was hammering away at the bunch of coolies, who, although they outnumbered him vastly, still held back as the lad shot ruthlessly.

Blake avoided a clinch. He wanted to keep his fists free, for he knew how much the result would be sheer chance should they go wrestling about among the roots and boles of the close-growing coco-nut trees. Rymer seemed content that this should be so, and surely never had those two fought a stranger battle than that night.

They could scarcely see each other, and yet each was making his blows tell. Blake, filled with burning rage as he realised how Rymer had thrown in his lot with a native bazaar dealer, and was actually out this night doing his dirty work, fought with a double purpose in mind.

Rymer, sore at heart and, vicious because he blamed Blake for upsetting his plans, was determined to make good his boast to Bamjee that he would "fix" the detective.

So it went on in ding-dong fashion; each man, a hard-hitting heavy-weight and no mean exponent of the art. They stumbled this way and that, the dull thud of their blows sounding with strange echoes under the trees.

Once Blake's heel caught in a root and he almost went down, but he managed to recover, although, as he came up, Rymer's fist caught him hard full in the face.

Blake gave way again, and then, as Rymer came on, he feinted and bored in like a fury. He got in under Rymer's guard, and, with his chin well down, drove in right and left with amazing rapidity in a tattoo to the body that sent Rymer back gasping.

Blake followed up his advantage and kept his man on the move until, as his back came against a tree, Rymer suddenly slipped round it, and before Blake could see in the gloom what had become of him, Rymer was round from the other side and upon him. It was just then that a crash sounded close to Blake's ear, and he realised that Tinker was still shooting.

The fight seemed to Blake to have lasted for ages, and he wondered in a fleeting way how the lad managed to keep his ammunition going. But, as a matter of fact, they had been hitting for less than five minutes, and that shot was Tinker's last. He was now into the remaining coolies with the butt of his weapon, and if Blake was fighting hard so was the lad.

But Rymer was in again; and this time Blake was forced to give way. Rymer followed him closely, placing each blow methodically and regularly. Blake seemed to become filled with a great lassitude. He could not understand himself. A few moments before he had been fighting as strong as possible, but now he could feel himself going down under the steady rain of wallops which Rymer was shooting in.

He made an effort to stand as he felt his shoulders touch a tree, but Rymer gave him no rest, and he came in now with a fury that seemed as if it would annihilate Blake.

Blake was still in a dazed condition. He had not noticed when one of Rymer's blows had caught him on the side of the neck, and he was therefore not aware that one of the positive nerves there had been momentarily paralysed. But he did know that his ancient enemy was going to whip him badly unless he made some change in the situation quickly. And then all of a sudden the pressure on the nerve was released.

New life seemed to flow back into him and, as he recovered, he drove into Rymer like a whirlwind. He asked no quarter, and gave none. Rymer, amazed at this sudden offensive on the part of one whom he thought he had already beaten, gave back under the hail of blows, and Blake gave him no rest.

Right, left, right, left he sent in wallop after wallop. It was impossible in that gloom to judge distance, but Blake made allowance for that, and made his blows too long rather than too short.

And then suddenly Rymer went down. Whether it was a blow that did the trick, or whether Rymer had tripped, he did not know. But as the big man stumbled back, Blake was on him, bore him to the earth, and, with one knee on his chest, shot in his hands for a throat hold.

Whether they wished it or not, they were forced to change their tactics, and now there was nothing of science about what followed. It was as primitive as if they had been two cave men in the early dawn of life, and each was filled with just as primitive a determination.

It was a terrible struggle that ensued. Neither of them knew that Tinker, sobbing with weakness, but victorious, was clinging to a tree close at hand, wanting to help but utterly incapable.

They did not even know what had happened to the coolies. They only knew that at last this thing must be settled to a finish, and they flung about like two snarling panthers while each fought to get the stranglehold on the other.

It could not go on for long. The pace was too terrific. It must end soon, and decisively. And it did. As they flung up against a tree, Blake squirmed round on top, and then, lifting his right fist, he smashed it down with all his remaining strength. He could not see Rymer's face, but he knew on the impact that he had aimed well.

The blow caught Rymer full in the mouth; he groaned with the agony of it, and his head rolled to one side. Blake struck again, and the third time he found the "button" at the point of the jaw. He felt Rymer collapse beneath him; felt his whole body relax, and knew his head had rolled to one side.

It was a knock-out, even if it wasn't a pretty one; and then, panting in great gasps, Blake staggered to his feet, to find Tinker staggering towards him, still flogging himself on to aid his master.

CHAPTER 16.   Blake Smashes the Plot—Conclusion.

BLAKE knew there was no further need of concealment now. In fact, there would be a good deal of publicity of necessity. So he resolved to go through with the thing as these new developments had forced him to handle it.

It took him only a short time to discover what the damage was among the natives— or, at least, among those who had been left. From the hut he got a light, and there on the bank were seven coolies wounded, more or less seriously. He saw with some relief that none had been killed. The rest had taken to flight under Tinker's attack, and the boats were nowhere to be seen.

He dragged up one who had been only slightly wounded in the arm, and pushed him forward. He ordered him to go through the trees to the other side of the island and hail one of the other munjis of which Rymer had spoken.

"You go across to Ernakulam," he told the coolie in Mallayalee, "and get hold of the doctor sahib there. Bring him here at once to attend to your fellows. If you fail to do this, I shall seek you out, and you will be severely punished. Do you understand?"

The native was all befogged at discovering this person who looked just like a coolie, too, was, in fact, a sahib, but he had had the fear of Shiva put in him, and he was only too ready to do as he was told. What the sahibs might be fighting about was none of his affair. He gave Tinker a wide berth, and started off; and then Blake turned his attention to Rymer.

He picked up his pistol, stuffed in a fresh clip, and, just as Rymer opened his eyes, Blake squatted over him, the pistol held in evidence so Rymer must see it in the glare of the light which Tinker was holding.

"Now we'll talk," said Blake grimly. "You came to 'settle' me, and bragged of what you were going to do. As the shoe is on the other foot, it is up to me to do the talking, so you will be wise to listen. Are you going to be reasonable?"

"I can't do anything else, can I," growled Rymer. "If I hadn't struck that cursed branch I'd have got you right enough. And I'll get you yet."

"Not this time, anyway," said Blake harshly. "Now, listen to me. I take it this little entertainment was cooked up by you and Bamjee?

You needn't stall on that—I know right enough the game you and Bamjee have been playing. You didn't think you could carry that on for ever without it being found out, did you?"

"Well, what of it?"

"Where is Green, the mycologist?" asked Blake with an abrupt change of the subject.

"Ask Bamjee," said Rymer.

"I thought so. I shall do that. You know, of course, what happened to Bamjee's relative last night."

"I know he was killed."

"Quite so. How much have you cleaned up, Rymer?"

"What has that to do with you?"

"I'll tell you. It was a great scheme, that. It needed a cunning native just like Bamjee to carry it out. And Bamjee needed you. You made a good team while the going was good. But Bamjee made a fool break—or you did—when Green was abducted. And it was another fool break to try that silly business last night. The native mind will always suffer from that defect. It never can grasp the mentality of the European. That poor fish thought he could drive me and Tinker out of the place by putting that harmless little owl on the roof—thought we would go because we would be tabooed. And you apparently agreed with him."

"No, I didn't!" snarled Rymer. "That is why I insisted on handling the thing my way."

"Like to-night, you mean. You did well, didn't you?"

"All right. My turn will come."

"Perhaps. But it won't come for some time if you go through to the Andamans over this job." (The Andaman Islands contain the Indian penal settlement in the Bay of Bengal.) "Now, I am going to say something to you, Rymer. You know as well as I do what you have done in mixing up with this native in such a contemptible plot. You have caused intense suffering to innocent natives, who could not afford to lose their crops of nuts.

"You know, too, that the truth can never be told to them. It would cause a rising along the whole coast, for the thing would become terribly exaggerated, and they would never believe that you did not get away with much more than you have secured. At the same time, I don't know how much you and Bamjee have cleaned up, but you are going to hand yours back. I shall realise on it, and see that the

111

proceeds reach those who have suffered. Also, you are going to clear out at once. I have got you where I want you, and I am going to smash you and Bamjee completely on this thing. If you don't agree to my terms, then I shall lift my hands and make a full statement to Government. I can promise you that if I do you will go to the Andamans as sure as my name is Sexton Blake. I haven't any time to waste, so you had better answer quick. Is it 'yes' or 'no'?"

"You've got me where you want me, so what else can I do but agree?" snarled Rymer. "I'll pay the price you ask. All I have got out of the deal is on the schooner. Come back there and I'll hand it over. And I don't care a hang what you do to Bamjee."

"I'll deal with Bamjee separately," promised Blake grimly.

They got Rymer into their own munji, and, while Tinker held him covered with the pistol, Blake paddled down the backwater to the schooner. They all went over the side, and Rymer led the way below to the saloon. Blake and Tinker kept close to his heels, and were beside him when he opened the door of one of the cabins and lit a lamp. Then he started across towards the bunk, but even as he did so he paused and gave vent to an exclamation. He lifted one arm and pointed to a gaping hole in the wall above the bunk.

"Gone!" he gasped. "There has been someone here. That is where I had the pearls, and they are gone!"

Blake started forward, but before he could say anything there was a sound at the door. They all turned to find Mary Trent standing there. She had just returned, and still held her sunshade in her hand. Her expression was non-committal as she gazed at them, but she had heard Rymer's last words, and she was quick enough to take in the situation. She knew, as well as if she had been told the details, that Rymer had come to hand grips with his old enemy that night, and had lost bad. And she knew, too, that Bamjee had planned the whole thing.

She looked at Tinker, then Blake, and finally Rymer.

"I take it they know?" she said at last.

Rymer nodded. Then Mary waved her hand behind her.

"If you look in the saloon you will find it in a state of confusion," she said. "The whole ship has been overhauled, and the searchers found the secret hiding-place, so it seems." Then, with a shrug: "I told you that native would double-cross you," she said, looking at Rymer.

Then all of a sudden he went berserk. For ten minutes he stormed and threatened, and tried to get out to seek out the dealer and vent his wrath on him. But Blake kept him forced back with the pistol, and at last Mary got him calmed down. But in his rage he had said all Blake needed to know of the full plot, and while Bamjee had made a clean search of the ship during the evening, Blake knew now about how much the pair of them had cleaned up on the scheme.

He had a talk with Mary Trent later, and, from what she told him, it was plain that Bamjee had figured on killing more than one bird with the same stone by setting Rymer on to Blake, and, while she was away from the schooner, getting all Rymer's share for himself. Blake said little to her about what had happened to him and Rymer. But he stuck to his word. He told her they must be out of the place by the morning, and that he would deal with Bamjee.

She agreed; and with that Blake and Tinker, still looking like a couple of coolies, dropped into the munji and paddled back to the hut on Bolghatty. They found the doctor from Ernakulam there, and saw that most of the wounded coolies had been already attended to. Blake and Tinker changed, and then, leaving the coolies to the doctor's care, they paddled across to Cochin.

Late though it was, Blake lost no time in getting to work, and that same night Bamjee's house was raided. They found the dealer alone in one of the rooms, and he did not offer any resistance to his arrest.

They rescued Green, who had been unharmed, and, when Bamjee realised that the game was up, he gave in completely, as all natives do. Blake forced out of him a confession as to the amount of gems he had received, and the box was handed to him.

Blake asked if Rymer's share was among them, but Bamjee protested that he knew nothing of them. Blake thought he was lying, and left it for the regular official to screw the truth out of him later, for he had already sent across for the state dewan to take charge of matters.

There is little more to tell. Bamjee was released on account of the very difficulty which Blake had found in dealing with Rymer. It would never do to let the ignorant coolie know the truth. The only thing was for the State to realise on the pearls and distribute the proceeds among the sufferers. And that was what was done.

Two days later Blake and Tinker took the train to Madras, and, as they went across the backwater, they saw that the white schooner was no longer at its anchorage opposite the mill. But Blake had already known he should not see it, for from the verandah of the bungalow—to which the servants had now returned—he had watched it beating down the coast just after dawn of the morning following the fight.

He would have been deeply interested had he been able to witness what was taking place on the poop deck of the schooner at that very moment when he saw it gleaming in the sun.

Rymer was at the wheel, staring moodily ahead. He was savage at being whipped by Blake, and he was savage at having all his weeks of work and scheming go for nothing. He had not spoken a word the whole night, and from time to time Mary had glanced at him with a curious expression in her eyes.

But she did not go near him until Cochin was being left behind. Then, however, she stole across to him and laid one arm across his shoulders.

"What is it, old boy?" she asked softly.

"You know well enough," he answered bitterly. "That cursed hound, Sexton Blake, and then to be double-crossed by a cheap-skate native."

Mary smiled full into his eyes.

"Who said he double-crossed you?" she asked.

"Why, he did. He rifled the whole schooner until he found the pearls. The dog!"

"I told you he would try to double-cross you, and he did—try," she rejoined. "But he did not succeed, my dear."

"Did not succeed! What do you mean, Mary?"

"Listen, old boy! Do you remember that I said I was going to send a souvenir to Anna Thurston yesterday afternoon?"

"Yes, you said something about it."

"Well, I sent it. I bought a sandalwood box and posted it to her yesterday afternoon. But that was not all. Before I went ashore I paid a secret visit to the place where you had the pearls hidden. I took them, all of them, and I put them in that box. At present they are on their way to Anna by registered post, and they could not be in a safer place than in the care of his Majesty's post. I felt that native would try and steal them, and he did, but —I stole them first!"

She laughed into his eyes, and, as Huxton Rymer realised how her quick wit had served him, he shot out one great arm and drew her in close to him.

"You—wonderful—girl!" he said into her hair, and the crimson stole up about her throat while the schooner lurched on across the blue Arabian Sea.

•   •   •   •   •

Two weeks later Sexton Blake and Tinker were pacing the deck of a homeward bound City Line boat. All of a sudden Blake stopped, and hit his hand against his thigh. Tinker watched in amazement while Blake turned and sped up to the deck above where the wireless operator held out. He sent off a long message to the sub-inspector at Cochin, the message to be relayed at Colombo. It was at Aden that he received a reply, and, as he read it, he laughed aloud.

"The cunning little creature!" he said. "What do you think, my lad?"

"What is it, guv'nor?"

"Do you recall that I sent a wireless off the other day?"

"Yes. You acted as if something had struck you."

"So it had. I have had a hunch all along that Mary Trent was pretty quick about saying that Bamjee had double-crossed Rymer. I have been thinking about that a lot, and all of a sudden I seemed to sense the truth."

"What was that, guv'nor?"

"That she had double-crossed the lot of us. And now I am positive she did. I sent a message to the sub-inspector asking him to make inquiries at the local post-office and find out if the European lady from the schooner had sent off anything on a certain date. Here is his reply. He says that she sent off a box by registered post on the afternoon of the date I named, and that it was given a nominal value of fifty pounds. If Rymer's pearls weren't in that box, then may I never take another case.

"Oh, those women! How is one to deal with them?"

And, still chuckling, Blake made for the smoking saloon, for that was the sort of a defeat that he could appreciate and enjoy.

THE END.
[48000 WORDS]

A GLOSSARY OF TERMS.

Pattimar.—A craft very much like the Arab dhow, which trades along the west coast of India, and from there across to the Persian Gulf. Exactly the same in type to-day as it was a thousand years or more ago.

Wallum.—A native boat, anything from fifteen to fifty feet in length, used for transporting produce (copra, coir yarn, pepper, ginger, etc.) in the backwaters of the Malabar coast.

Munji.—A little native dugout, and very "tricky."

Bandicoot.—A form of super-rat found in India and the East. It is a very vicious brute, and when cornered will fight like fury. Its bite is very dangerous, for it feeds practically only on the worst forms of offal.

Mali.—Native term for gardener.

Punkah-man.—The servant who pulls the "punkah," or length of matting which is hung on a verandah or in a room to keep the air cool where electric fans cannot be had.

Chokra.—Young native servant, assistant to the butler, or "boy,"

Shikari. A hunter or a guide

State Diwan or Dewan.—First or Prime Minister to the Maharajah or Itaja of any native state.

Maidan. — an open space in or near a town, used as a parade ground or for events such as public meetings.

Mycologist.—Attached to the Agricultural Department of any district in order to make a scientific study of the diseases of plants and trees.

Chota Nazra or Nazri.—Usually the former, means first, or little, breakfast. Chota, little; nazra, food of early day.

COPRA

Many writers have referred to the sago palm as the greatest gift which Nature has made to man, for from that prolific and generous tree the native of the South Sea Islands can gain practically everything he needs to feed and clothe and house himself. But it is scarcely to be ranked higher than the coco-nut palm in that respect, for therein is proof of the bounty which Nature has showered upon her children.

The trunks give him building timber and the leaves give him a roof. The nut gives him food and drink, and from the husk he gets a fibre of quality from which he can make his fishing nets and ropes for a thousand purposes, from the fruit he can draw a sap, which gives him the wonderfully refreshing "toddy"—a wonderful drink, when it can be secured fresh from the tree and before the heat of the day has turned it to the regular arrack of the bazaars.

Not a long list that, but many more items could be added. But the one which has meant more to the white man than any other is the dried white meat of the nut, known throughout the world as copra.

Wherever the coco-nut grows there does one find copra—not the meat which one sees in the homely coco-nut of the country fair "shy," but dried beneath a tropic sun for from six to eight days, until nearly every drop of water moisture has been drawn out. Nothing is left then but the white meat, of which the oil content amounts to anything from sixty-five to eighty per cent, and it is this oil which goes in its hundreds and thousands of tons to the great factories, where soap and margarine are made.

The South Sea Islands produce a very large quantity each year, but there the handling is not on a very enlightened basis and a good many of the cargoes picked up by the island trading schooners are rancid and only fit for the coarsest soaps by the time they reach the home market. West Africa, too, produces some, but there the growers and shippers specialise more on palm kernels. From Ceylon comes some of the best copra grown, but ranking high above all others is the sun-dried copra of the Malabar coast of India. That copra invariably commands anything from £1 to £2 10s. per ton more than any other on the market.

Not all the copra brought in by the natives is shipped as such. On the contrary. In the Philippine Islands, in Ceylon, and in Malabar vast quantities are crushed locally, sometimes in modern up-to-date mills, with hydraulic presses, such as one finds throughout the Philippines (and from there, in fact, scarcely any actual copra is shipped, as the Americans export most of it as oil in big tank steamers) and Ceylon and the native "chuck" presses of Malabar.

In that case the residue, which is called "poonac," is a by-product of some value, for it is a very useful cattle food and, in some cases is most useful as a fertiliser. To show a sidelight on the efficiency of the Germans it will serve to relate what used to happen before the war. In Malabar, from the native chuck presses the poonac used to contain something like thirteen per cent of oil after the pressing. This was bought up eagerly by the Germans and for a long time no one could understand just why it was that Hamburg and Bremen always paid a much higher price for Malabar "poonac" than any other ports. Well, some German scientist discovered that in feeding "poonac" to cattle only a very small percentage of the oil content was actually absorbed by the animal, that it did not need being thrown off in the usual way. This scientist figured that no animal ever took more than six per cent, and seldom that. So, before using the poonac as cattle food he showed how seven or eight per cent, of the oil content could be precipitated by a chemical process, (some form of benzine bath) and then the poonac was resold to the cattle food dealers at the regular price, while the oil was barrelled and sold at the market price for that commodity, which was, of course, four or five times higher than the price of poonac!

The coco-nut tree is looked upon by the average native with veneration and, like any other bit of property is handed down from one generation to another, for it is a vigorous bearing tree up to the age of a hundred. Indeed the trunk does not come to its best for building purposes until the tree is forty years old, and in Malabar, when a bit of land changes hands, from one native to another, the average value put on each tree and paid is two hundred rupees—a matter of a little over £13. And a few trees of that value mean a lot to the little grower, with about a tenth of an acre of ground, whose earnings, when he does work, amount to the munificent sum of the equivalent of two-pence a day—and he isn't always worth that!

Afterward

The process of capture and research on this book was very enjoyable. The physical size of this 1925 English magazine/novel, really a 'pulp', is diminutive at 5.5 by 7 inches. The font size is remarkable at Century Schoolbook 7 font, and thinking that eyeglasses were probably very expensive, I believe the format might have been dictated by the recent end of the war and a general scarcity of materials.

The popularity of these adventures probably cannot be compared since the only major media of the time was print.

On Coconut Pearls

Fifty years ago, I read *Wonder Plants and Plant Wonders* (1939) by A. Hyatt Verrill. This great read caused our Family to visit the Tropics and further research on their amazing plants. Verrill refers to *The Tropical Crops* (1928) by Otis Warren Barrett, a specialist. Having read these, it seems astonishing that there was never a mention of Coconut Pearls! It is notable that the scientific report in *Nature*, mentioned in Wiki, was published in January 1925!

Perhaps the reason is that they don't really exist? An archive of the Wikipedia entry for 'coconut pearls' was created just because the page may not be displayed much longer!

I hope you enjoyed this read as much as I did.

Doug Frizzle
March 2019.

https://www2.palomar.edu/users/warmstrong/ww0601c.htm
This is a long document; search on 'pearl'.

https://en.wikipedia.org/wiki/Coconut_pearl
The **current** Wiki page
also archived, just-in-case...
    https://web.archive.org/web/20190318112856/https://en.wikipedia.org/wiki/Coconut_pearl

www.ingramcontent.com/pod-product-compliance
Lightning Source LLC
Chambersburg PA
CBHW052207170626
46812CB00004B/1690